Inside the Tower heat and pressure gauges passed their redlines and finally hit their limits.

Angus 7873 was with Monica 2488 out in front of the fleeing soldiers. Calvin 6501 was close behind with the other Attackers.

The ridge crest was in sight.

Thirty meters.

Twenty.

Ten.

Over it. Angus stumbled.

Fell. Rolled down the slope.

Calvin 6501 cleared it. The others followed clumsily.

The last Attackers and Defenders ran in the dark night as fast as they could, nearing the ridge.

The Tower was now a...

A WORD ON TERRAFORMING

NASA, the National Aeronautics and Space Administration, has had plans for several years to TERRAFORM Mars. The technology exists to increase Mars' natural greenhouse gases in an effort to melt its polar ice caps, creating oceans that will make Mars a livable planet like Earth. In short, forming a dead planet into something like "Terra," Earth.

Throughout history profit has been the number one motivator for all technologies. Without a civic voice of leadership saying something like "within this decade, we will land a man on the moon," it falls to corporations to push the technological envelope and express their will.

As humanity achieves real space travel, an immediate outcome will be that huge corporations will take over efforts that are currently managed by governmental agencies. The combination of a feeble appreciation for human life, advanced technologies, and the pursuit of corporate profits could naturally result in situations such as described in the following pages...

OXYGEN
WARS

OXYGEN WARS

A Novel

by

MELTON EDUARDO CARTES

Oxygen Wars

AlbinoPigGorilla Press

For information:
www.meltoncartes.com
www.albinopiggorilla.com

ISBN 978-0-578-40577-3

Printed in the United States of America

DEDICATION

This book is dedicated to those who still think
that war is a viable alternative and who, in pursuit of
profit, have lost track of the value of human life.

ACKNOWLEDGEMENTS

Oxygen Wars is an idea that first took form as a screenplay with the collaboration of my friend and frequent writing partner Daniel Merritt. Jonathan Hennessey also deserves thanks for thoroughly getting the intention behind this story as well as championing it whenever he has had a chance. As time goes by, this concept gathers more and more pertinence, particularly as the world becomes more aware of the privatization of security and military forces.

TABLE OF CONTENTS

OXYGEN WARS

THE DISTANT FUTURE...

THE DIRT PLANET

Angus 7873 lay where he had fallen, inactive, eyes closed. The most critical damage he had sustained in the battle was to his antenna hump, the communication center of his suit; it was shorted out by the blast from the Flying Vehicle. The rest of his damage consisted of the typical bumps, dents and scrapes acquired in battle.

He and the others now lay under sand, buried by the wind as it blew over them.

The silent Tower complex remained that way into twilight, looming over them and the littered battlefield around it. Trailing smoke and a few desultory sparks and fires provided the only detectable movement on the scene. As the sky darkened, a heavier gloom fell over the scattered bodies that previously seemed so formidable.

But a shadow jiggled behind a boulder a step away from the fallen soldier. Slowly, timidly, a squat shape — only a few inches high — peeked out. It was a small service robot with a cluster of tiny eyes, legs and claws. It tested the air like a field mouse sniffing for predators. It seemed to determine that conditions were safe and scurried out into the open.

The crab-like robot picked its way over to another fallen Attacker, Carter 3440. A soldering device deployed from the "crab's" body, illuminating the engraved designation on its surface; P-Vo/31417800001430709741209897012 3431072343. Its full name was extremely long for such a tiny creature, unless it were shortened to P-Vo. It started to weld one of Carter 3440's dislodged armor plates that hung at an angle, back onto his body, inadvertently making his leg stir and kick reflexively.

As P-Vo worked happily, more repair crabs began to emerge from every cubbyhole on the entire battlefield. Most came from the downed soldiers; they normally stowed away in sconces and cubicles built into the armor. Others lay dormant in the surrounding sand or in the Tower complex, apparently waiting for a job. Thousands of them emerged, all of them making repairs or salvaging parts from those too far gone.

One soldier had been split in half from a direct hit, her human half liquefied from exposure to the atmosphere. But her mechanical half still retained a basic physical integrity. In a short time what started as a smattering of curious repair crabs became a crowd and then a swarm as they collected around her fallen body. They went to work dismantling the bulky suit of armor and, like ants, they worked together to lift masses many, many times larger and heavier than themselves. They quickly separated a leg from the rest and carried it off to the side where it too was broken down into smaller pieces that could be used by the different work crews that had formed out of this project. In this way, the fallen soldier's remains slowly exploded over the surface of the sand, her different parts going to serve their new purposes elsewhere. As quickly as these workers assembled, they dispersed to other tasks, leaving the human body to complete its decomposition in this caustic environment.

The battlefield shimmered in the twilight with the movements of thousands of repair crabs. Here and there, larger pieces would suddenly rear up from the sand and rotate or pivot as the many workers maneuvered them to their benefit. Like a beehive, the battlefield was a swarm of activity and purpose.

One regiment of tough little crabs formed around P-Vo as they focused on one area of Carter 3440's damage. In perfect sequence they hammered a mangled armor plate back into shape. Almost brand new.

Carter 3440's running lights re-ignited. His data screens filled and immediately displayed the suit's diagnostic routines. Images and text played spookily over his face, and then his eyes opened.

Carter 3440's arms and legs pumped awkwardly, as if recalling their functions, and then chose specific positions for leverage. He pushed himself up and rolled over, trapping several crabs beneath himself in the sand as the rest hung on or fell off and scurried away. He then got to his feet and, after some more contemplation, practiced some quick draws with his various weapons.

He let out a strange, mechanical yawn and then spoke, "Buddha? Carter reporting one hundred percent rehab and ready." In a moment he received a response signal and with that he started to wander away.

That Angus 7873 on some level was aware of all of this activity was unlikely. Whatever was going through his mind was a mystery to all but himself. Given the symbiotic nature of his human and machine halves and his state of inactivity, he too was probably unaware of his own thoughts. Not blissful, but ignorant.

But some thoughts had to be coursing through all of those synapses and neurons and nerves. He wasn't dead and the brain loves to think. It loves to think about anything; abstractions or practicalities. It thinks about details and broad strokes. It thinks about the past, present and future. But most of all it likes to think about the past, memories. Memories are the cobblestones that pave the way. They give context and sometimes meaning. They may not explain everything, but they fill the mind with enough stuff to make one think that things make sense, even if they don't.

Some may think that memories are personal. They're not. Like cobblestones, they're just moments that come along and then pass. Those moments that are then stored away as imperfect recollections, faulty evidence of an experience, become memories.

Sunlight is impersonal. It falls upon its subjects indifferently, but it's never stingy. It provides life and death in equal measure. Although that measure is averaged out, making life and death more common in one era as opposed to another.

Out of billions of stars, this single star shined its light on a smattering of planets accreted to its side. One of these planets rotated to a new day as its dead atmosphere swirled in complaint and disturbance, as if this once vital and fertile planet still held a grudge for having become barren. Now it was just an angry red orb of sand, rock and caustic gases that no longer sustained life, circulating endlessly.

As this sun shined over this rugged world the thin atmosphere fluoresced, acknowledging its existence. It was a feeble atmosphere, alternating between red and blue hues, depending on the angle of the sunlight.

Tempests and currents swirled noxious clouds across its face, creating a distressed, streaked pattern as the weather gouged millions of years of texture more deeply into the planet's surface. It was an angry red orb.

A geostationary satellite seemed to fly by in its orbit, in sync with the planet's surface, forever locked above a single location. As part of a network of satellites, it relayed information and commands to other parts of this dreary world. Even though this looked like a dead place, even though this looked like a desolate planet, there were inhabitants on this world and those commands were meant for them.

The turbulent atmosphere's chief agent was wind. It bullied across the planet surface molding and shaping the land, clearing and obscuring areas, periodically howling and singing its own praises. Nothing else would.

The wind churned up a dust devil, a cyclone of dirt, that twisted over the land, picking up more soil, obscuring the landscape with its passage. What normally would be a distinct plain or mountain ridge or plateau was now an indistinct gray mass, made vague by a haze limiting visibility to a short distance. The wind continued to carom over the land, slowly clearing what it obscured.

The broken terrain peeked through. Craggy ridges and cliffs stood out against the rust-colored sky. Passing clouds of dust hid and revealed more of the landscape.

A massive silhouette showed through the haze: a vertical projection of some sort. It was not part of the rocky ridge that curtained this area; its nature was distinct, a different material, another design. It cropped up just before the ridge, inside its perimeter, sheltered by it.

A heartier gust of wind cleared the haze, revealing the shape to be a building. It was a huge tower of steel and concrete that stood there for an unknown length of time. The Tower was a huge conical cylinder with a fluted top much like the old containment towers of nuclear power plants. As more of the dust cleared away, it became clear that the Tower was part of a bigger complex with smaller towers and structures complementing it. This complex stood as a sentinel looking out at the deserted and windswept plain, as if it were protecting the rocky cliffs behind it.

Another group of structures stood in a row on a nearby ridge still obscured by the swirling dust and sand. But as the wind swept this away as well, it showed them for what they were. Soldiers.

Scores of them stood or sat in huddles, waiting. They faced downwind from the storm waiting for it to pass.

FIGHTING

These soldiers were humans encased in armor that augmented them to nearly three times their size. Their heads were centered inside glass spheres that contained the atmosphere they needed to survive. These armored suits were aged and beaten collections of salvaged parts and welded patches, creating a patina of history with the resulting texture. Add to that corrosion and the faded remnants of painted markings and corporate logos and their appearance became a dense collection of details giving these figures an almost baroque quality.

As rich in detail as the metal surfaces of these figures were, their human insides were devoid of character or expression, except for a basic look of exhaustion. As the wind subsided and the air cleared, one of these figures turned around to look at the complex.

The man inside this armor was no longer young, but not old either. His head was hairless and his face was sunken by the same exhaustion as the others. His was the face of mental inactivity. This man wasn't stupid. He simply had no need for any thoughts other than those coursing through him at that moment that were purely autonomic, concerned with the simple functions of his body and his armored suit. He adjusted his posture as the wind shoved him.

Inside his helmet of glass and metal a minor alarm went off, triggering a scheduled diagnostic test. He raised his arm and with it an intimidating weapon swiveled into his hand, cycled through loading functions and then chimed its readiness. It was a laser cannon as well as rocket and grenade launcher, supported on a counter-balanced articulated extension attached to his back and positioned right under his right arm. The extension retracted the cannon and returned to a ready position. Satisfied, this soldier returned to his position of rest and waiting. Some of the other soldiers also made similar adjustments and preparations, but all of them continued to wait, patient as the stones around them.

Unlike the rest, this one soldier's lips began moving unconsciously as he muttered a single phrase, "...look for the blue sky..."

The inside of his helmet consisted of an array of data monitors and measurement devices which displayed pertinent information related to the functions of his body and his armor. Periodically a full-body diagnostic screen would appear on different screens labeling this particular soldier as: Angus - 7873.

Angus 7873 waited.

Soldiers were the same throughout the universe, extremely ordinary in extraordinary situations. These soldiers were unremarkable except perhaps in their ability to wait. They had been waiting for days on this ridge and they would wait for many more days if necessary. All of them had alerts on their screens telling them why they were waiting, until now. Something had changed, a small company of other soldiers had arrived from wandering the planet and the balance of power had suddenly shifted.

Angus 7873's eyes looked up anticipating movement. Massive sliding doors at the base of the Tower slowly parted. Lights blinked on in the Tower's darker interior. The lights seemingly moved with purpose toward the open door as more and more lights came on.

As the lights moved out of the Tower they revealed themselves to be lamps, headlights on the helmets of soldiers that were identical in form and makeup to those waiting on the ridge. With the introduction of this new element, the basic nature of the waiting soldiers changed as they now clearly became the attacking force. They shifted their weight and fidgeted, like the nervous horses before the Charge of the Light Brigade in a far-off time. Again Angus 7873 muttered "Look for the blue sky,..." but louder this time and with more meaning.

All of the Attackers heard a chime in their helmets and joined in chorus, "Look for the blue sky."

The Attackers fanned out swiftly, taking their positions remarkably quickly for their bulk. Angus 7873 opened his mouth again, tentatively, and uttered, "Tycho Buddha. Defender response. Defender response." His mechanically processed voice communicated to all of the helmets in the vicinity. From one moment to the next change happened instantly on this world, or not at all.

A beam of light slices from the open doors and hits the Attacker standing next to Angus 7873, dead center, blowing her into pieces. Angus 7873 doesn't flinch as pieces bounce off of him and the others. More beams of light slice out of the Tower's dark interior.

Angus 7873's face is illuminated by a flashing light inside his helmet. Two of his data screens flash "ATTACK MODE," indicating that he and the other soldiers who had been waiting are now working in concert.

Angus 7873 and his fellow Attackers watch as the figures inside the Tower's base slowly emerge into the

Dirt Planet's poison-colored sunlight. These are the Defenders, charged with protecting the Tower complex. The Attackers wait a few moments more, as if in observance of regimental protocol such as soldiers of another bygone era.

Then inside all of the Attackers' helmets a coded response sounds in a purely mechanical language. The effect on Angus 7873 and all of his comrades is significant. Pupils dilate. Eyes focus. Weight shifts forward. Angus 7873 shoulders his heavy cannon, attached to his side by the articulated counter-weighted extension, takes a deep breath, and yells, "LOOK FOR THE BLUE SKY!!!"

Change happens instantly on this planet, or not at all. Explosions. Shrieking gunfire. Lasers slicing through the air. Smoke, sand and debris. Some Defenders fall. Injured. Dead.

Angus 7873 reports, "Four Defenders. One dead." Another Attacker, with his scarred and chipped designation on one shoulder identifying him as Spelvin 2283, pauses amid the fighting and looks at Angus 7873. "One. Correction. Two Attackers down," he reports.

Grenades land near Spelvin 2283. Another Attacker behind him is blown into fragments. Spelvin 2283 doesn't even have to turn around to see what happened: data screens in his suit constantly update information. "Three Attackers terminus," Spelvin 2283 says.

Angus 7873 wheels around and fires at Roach 9901,

a Defender, but only scores a glancing blow. Roach 9901 turns on him, muttering, "Miss." He fires a warhead-tipped rocket at Angus 7873.

Angus 7873 staggers to the side: the rocket clangs as it glances off his armor without detonating. It bounces off the ground, kicking up broken rock before exploding in the air. The concussion shoves Angus 7873 and others, forcing them to adjust their footing. Angus 7873 fires another burst at his enemy. His shot tears Roach 9901's transparent faceplate off his helmet. Roach 9901 gasps, stunned. "No! No! Help! Help!..." Roach 9901 cries.

Roach 9901's lungs fill with the planet's atmosphere as he gasps without his protective helmet. Immediately he drops his weapons on their articulated arms and starts to convulse. Angus 7873 watches as Roach 9901's skin starts to sizzle and break into weeping blisters. Blood leaks from his eyes, nose and ears freely.

Angus 7873 stares at him impassively. But a slight facial tic might suggest something more.

Roach 9901 falls, screaming in human pain. As he starts to die he reaches out to the Tower he had been defending. "Tycho Muhammad, forgive me.... Help me,..." he gasps. Roach 9901 dies staring at the Tower and corrodes right in front of Angus 7873 as the battle rages around them.

Angus 7873 turns and stares at the Tower. It looks like Angus 7873 and his Attackers are winning the battle. Spelvin 2283 reports, "Tycho Buddha. Penetrate Tower perimeter."

"Excellence. Breach imminent." Angus 7873 responds.

"Negative. Negative breach imminent." Angus 7873 turns and sees Calvin 6501 bearing down on them. Angus 7873's eyes flick over Calvin 6501's armor. The remnants of logos dapple his armor: GeoConSo. Angus 7873 and Spelvin 2283 react.

Calvin 6501 unloads a particle beam on Spelvin 2283. It's a direct hit: Spelvin 2283 explodes. But suddenly Calvin 6501 comes under heavy fire and has to back away. Angus 7873 stares at the name painted on Calvin 6501's armor.

Angus bears a collage of logos, but at one time he belonged to PetroCom, according to the logo that is oldest and most prominent on his armor. He turns to engage another pocket of Defenders trying to regroup, his thoughts back on the battle.

Calvin 6501 surveys his followers falling all around him. He turns and looks at the Tower. "Tycho Muhammad. Defender rank declining, 30%. Require air support," Calvin 6501 announces. He blinks and then a coded response sounds in his helmet.

"Blessings from Muhammad," Calvin 6501 says.

Indeed, the Attackers have managed to capitalize on an early advantage and threaten to breach the Tower complex. There are slightly more Attackers as Defenders.

But, casualties have evened out those numbers.

The Tower complex is in a basin backed against the cliff wall. This forces the battle to be head-on and hard-fought. Despite their skill the Defenders are easier targets.

Angus 7873 sees an opening in the fighting and starts to move toward it. His attention is drawn by something in the sky. He looks up and sees a Flying Vehicle banking around the battle. Angus 7873's faceplate shades him from the sun, helping him see the vehicle. It has wings and stabilizers and ramjet intakes and exhaust ports that swivel with instant and minute corrections as it slows to a hover overhead.

And then hell rains down from it. Angus 7873 watches as multiple particle beams fire from the Flying Vehicle. Initially the shots miss, forcing the Attackers to alter their actions. Then Attackers everywhere are blown to pieces. Angus 7873 scrambles to take cover.

The Flying Vehicle is on the side of the Defenders. Its firepower is impressive. It's powerful and accurate. Its position is cruelly advantageous. These formidable fighting machines are made ridiculous by this heavenly threat. Many Attackers are destroyed completely, their parts scattered over the field. Others are merely injured, damaged and put out of commission as far as fighting is concerned. In a short time the Flying Vehicle reduces the threat to the Tower, neutralizing the attack.

The Flying Vehicle flies around at will. At times it swoops like a bird. At other times it flits to and fro like a huge dragonfly. This planet had never before seen birds or dragonflies. But the Flying Vehicle seems to be at home here.

Angus 7873 is one of the last Attackers left standing. A bolt from the Flying Vehicle just misses him. Despite his size, he moves fast. He stops. The Flying Vehicle roars past to turn around and make another pass. "Tycho Buddha. Heavy casualties. Withdraw. Withdraw." Angus 7873 reports with panic welling up in his throat.

He starts to run back toward the ridge they came from.

But, Calvin 6501 rams his armor into Angus 7873, like a body check. Angus 7873 whirls around to square off with Calvin 6501. Calvin 6501 raises his laser cannon to point it at Angus 7873. But Angus 7873 knocks it aside with one arm and punches him in the faceplate with his other arm.

Calvin 6501 stumbles backward and then spins around using his new center of gravity to regain his footing and face his opponent. Angus 7873 aims his cannon at Calvin 6501; now it's Calvin 6501's turn to swat a laser cannon aside.

Angus 7873 reaches out and grabs Calvin 6501's weapon to keep him from using it. They grapple, hand to hand, and try to throw each other off balance.

The Flying Vehicle circles back to get a better shot at

Angus 7873. It slows to a hover over the mad wrestling match between the two armored soldiers. It adjusts its position minutely, looking for a shot. Its weapons project from various places on the fuselage. The whole time the Flying Vehicle fires harrying shots at other parts of the battlefield. But it's struggling to get a shot at Angus 7873 without hitting Calvin 6501. Each time it seems to be ready to fire, it retracts its barrels and recalculates.

Angus 7873 and Calvin 6501 struggle and pivot. The Flying Vehicle spins around in mid-air following their movements closely. The combatants manage to flip each other in a show of incredible ferocity and strength. The Flying Vehicle adjusts its altitude and angle, but no matter what it does, it can't get a clear shot. Finally the Flying Vehicle seems to pause for a moment, rather than follow each movement of the fighting soldiers.

The Flying Vehicle's aim adjusts. A beam turns the ground white behind Angus 7873. The resulting blast sends both soldiers flying end over end into a ravine.

Even as he hurtles, Angus 7873 tries to communicate. "TYCH#@...DDHA. TYCHO*S!BUDKL!" Behind his neck the antenna hump of his telemetry pack crackles as it burns out. Sparks fly from it. Angus 7873 smashes into the side of the ravine. A singed Calvin 6501 flops near him with equal violence, apparently dead.

The Flying Vehicle dodges twice, as if checking its handiwork. Apparently satisfied, it climbs higher and does a circuit of the battlefield, firing harassing shots intermittently without causing any more real damage. Further satisfied, the Flying Vehicle stops firing, completes its final circuit and flies off in the direction it came.

Smoke trails from the injured and dead soldiers, Attackers and Defenders, scattered around the mouth of the Tower complex.

Silence.

The battle was over.

Angus 7873 lay where he had fallen, inactive, eyes closed. His armor was ripped up. Burned.

Attackers and Defenders littered the entire landscape. Lost appendages, dropped weapons, spent mortar shells and land mine debris covered the battlefield. The Flying Vehicle had neutralized the fighting and the few remaining Defenders walked back into the Tower, leaving behind their dead.

It was an angry red orb.

AWAKENING

More crabs pulled the dead Defender, Roach 9901, out of his armor and broke it up for the spare parts. In a remarkably short amount of time, these tiny creatures expertly disassembled the armor, cables and surgical tubing. Teams of crabs tugged on IVs, sliding them out of Roach 9901's arms and legs. The dead man was discarded like a snail out of its shell. Fully exposed to the corrosive atmosphere, the rest of Roach 9901's body smoldered and degraded, becoming a steaming puddle pooled around his skeleton.

Repair crabs similarly swarmed over Spelvin 2283's suit. One detached itself, dragged several pieces from other downed soldiers, and made a slow but sure beeline to Angus 7873.

P-Vo was already there, trying to work on the burnt-out antenna hump at Angus 7873's neck. A group of crabs repaired and replaced the rest of the antenna hardware and left, leaving the old antenna hump a hunk of melted alloys lying in the sand.

But P-Vo couldn't seem to get the new circuit board to work in the repaired antenna hump. P-Vo went over to the new crab that had just joined and picked through the spare parts it brought over. There was another communications board, from Spelvin 2283, that looked just like Angus 7873's. The two crabs got into a short, nasty tug-of-war over it. But finally, P-Vo won. It dragged the communications board over and switched them. But as P-Vo's appendages poked, prodded and soldered, the new communications board crackled and sparked and burned out. P-Vo backed away, spooked.

And then it stared.

Finally, it slumped. It sealed a panel over the burnt out circuit board and scrambled away to its next job, leaving Angus 7873's fate to other crabs.

Over all of this the Tower stood conceitedly, illuminated by spotlights. Millions of tiny lights swarmed the battlefield. The repair crabs busily worked under the gaze of the Tower and twin moons in the sky. The salvage operations stretched into the night.

As the sun came up over the battlefield the next day

more of the debris had been cleared and here and there soldiers were standing up and wandering away.

Another soldier stirred, her name, Hagen 6460, barely legible through scars and burns on her armor. The human being inside was a haggard veteran of many battles. Her right arm and left leg stirred again as she lay face down in the sand. Repair crabs emerged from tunnels they had dug underneath her and crawled all over, going about their business.

Her suit came on and went through the diagnostic routine. Her facial expressions seemed to go from dead sleep to consciousness as the diagnosis processed to an end and her eyes opened.

She pushed herself up to her feet and did the same mechanical yawn followed by, "Buddha? Hagen reporting one hundred percent rehab and ready." She then received the same response signal Carter 3440 received. Hagen 6460 got up and wandered away with her laser cannon at port.

Six or seven repair crabs carried a piece of armor to Spelvin 2283. The crabs stopped, thought better of it, turned and carried the armor to Angus 7873 where they immediately welded it on him as a patch.

Angus 7873 stirred. The diagnostic routine began as his suit came on. His face went through the same series of expressions as the mind behind it slowly woke. The many nuances of expressions shifted almost imperceptibly from one to another, sometimes manifesting solely as twitches and tics. The diagnostic routine finished and Angus 7873 opened his eyes and sat up.

Parts of Spelvin 2283's helmet lay near Angus 7873. He stared at it with a blank expression on his face and waited. Calvin 6501 stirred next to him, having gone through the same process, and yawned in the same mechanical way as Carter 3440. "Buddha? Calvin 6501 reporting one hundred percent rehab and ready," he uttered. Calvin 6501 got the acknowledgement signal and then stood up. Angus 7873's attention was drawn to him as he stood and tested his appendages one final time. Nearby, crabs were dismantling Spelvin 2283's parts.

Angus 7873 looked at his own data screen readouts: `99.99973% rehab and ready.` He studied the other soldiers standing up here and there who were beginning their new wanderings. The anomaly was obvious and his thoughts, the organic as well as the augmented ones, turned to figuring it out. Using what little autonomy he had, Angus 7873 spoke, saying, "Buddha? Angus reporting ninety-nine point nine, nine, nine, seven, three percent rehab and ready." He waited. "Buddha? Angus reporting ninety-nine point nine, nine, nine, seven, three percent rehab. Ready. Respond," he reiterated.

Angus 7873 struggled to his feet as half of the

response signal came through. It almost sounded interrogative compared to the other response signals. Angus 7873 frowned. "Incomplete," he said.

Angus 7873 looked at the data screens inside his helmet. Following an internal instruction, a smaller hand came out of the palm of his larger augmented and armored hand and operated a keypad on the forearm of his other arm. "Re-send," he said. Calvin 6501 looked at him with a bored expression.

The acknowledgement came through again, eighty percent of it. Angus hit his helmet with one hand — mechanical gremlins and quirks being one other intangible, but known, inhabitant of this deserted planet. He looked at all of his data screens. Nothing. No warning. No malfunction. He typed a new combination and one of his data screens showed: `Repair Mode, COMMLINK`.

Angus 7873's suit performed another self-diagnosis, ultimately displaying: `COMMLINK - 100% integrity`. Angus 7873's mind struggled to shift gears in the face of this dilemma. He was for all intents and purposes repaired and ready for duty. But the crucial last step was incomplete, communicating his ready status to Buddha. Calvin 6501 stared obliviously at Angus 7873 in his predicament. Because he was standing in front of him, Angus 7873 stared back at Calvin 6501. Calvin 6501 started to turn away to begin his wandering.

Angus 7873's eyes darted around his data screens

searching for an option, a work-around. One of his data screens displayed the surrounding terrain and objects. The closest thing of course was Calvin 6501, not counting the thousands of repair crabs that still scurried about. The data screen displayed a diagram and the official designation of Calvin 6501. "Calvin 6501," Angus 7873 said.

For his part Calvin 6501 simply stared out into space and said, "Tycho Muhammad. Vector seventeen das twenty eight, Orlando." Angus 7873 cocked his head slightly in consternation. "Calvin 6501. Tycho Buddha. Ready," Angus 7873 said. Perhaps Calvin 6501 could relay his message. Calvin 6501 stared at Angus without reaction. Angus 7873 tried numerous variations of communication protocols. "Tycho Buddha. Tycho Buddha. Ready."

Calvin 6501 turned around and walked away. Calvin 6501 wandered away in the same direction as the others. But Angus 7873 wanted him to wait. "Calvin 6501. Calvin 6501. Tycho Buddha. Tycho Buddha. Ready. Ready," Angus 7873 repeated nervously. Despite his deadened affect, Angus 7873's voice rose in pitch, indicating a growing anxiety. But Calvin 6501 ignored him. Angus 7873 got more worked up. "...wait," Angus 7873 pleaded.

Angus 7873 watched as one by one all of the rehabilitated soldiers disappeared over the horizon. Angus 7873 desperately tried to communicate with someone, anyone. The more they ignored him the higher his voice got and the more quickly Angus 7873 spoke. Angus 7873 seemed unused to making the facial expressions that were occurring on his face. "...Tycho Buddha sta..." Angus 7873 faltered. "Tycho Buddha sta..." Angus 7873 faltered again.

Angus 7873 just watched as the last soldier on the plain became a dot on the horizon. After a while the dot blinked out of existence, leaving Angus 7873 very much alone.

Angus 7873 blinked and frowned, confused. The slide show of emotions played on his face as Angus 7873 seemed to go from plain thought to anxiety and back to plain thought while standing there. Long pauses interrupted these emotional moments, where Angus 7873 just stared out of his helmet. The whole time Angus 7873 repeated his communication, waiting for an acknowledgement, "Tycho Buddha. Ready."

And then a familiar emotion crept up on him that Angus 7873 previously had only known in battle.

SEPARATION

"Tycho reticuli Buddha?" Angus 7873 waited for an answer.

"Tycho reticuli Buddha?" No one responded. The sun dropped below the horizon, leaving him in the growing gloom trying to connect.

The twilight sky created a murk around the few rocks that stuck out of the surrounding sand. As Angus 7873's eyes scanned the area, it became harder for him to distinguish details. Angus 7873's headlamps turned on automatically and cast bright pools of white light wherever he looked, wiping out the twilight gloom, but providing little more in helpful data.

Then all of Angus 7873's data screens flashed red

alerts. His bio readouts were spiking alarmingly as Angus 7873 grimaced. His eyes opened wide and his gaze darted about the empty terrain searching more desperately for something Angus 7873 couldn't have identified.

"Buddha?" Angus 7873 hissed. He repeated more forcefully, "BUDDHA?" The terrain remained quiet and indifferent. Angus 7873 then hollered, "Buddha? Buddha? Buddha?" There was no response as he stumbled forward and his hands rose in a plaintive, searching gesture.

"Buddha? Buddha?" Angus 7873 said as he lurched in a spiral, a basic search pattern for finding something lost. He continued, gradually widening his circles as if he were simply scanning the surroundings, like the sweep of a radar. "Buddha?" Angus 7873 pleaded over and over. As he spiraled and called out, a cry gradually emerged from him.

At first it was just a whimpering little sound, a complaint, a thought out loud. But as Angus 7873 stumbled about his whimpering became a bona fide wail. The only times Angus 7873 had ever wailed, or could remember having wailed, were moments of stark terror in battle.

This was not battle. This was just the darkness of nighttime in the barren desert on this ruthless planet; a night like a million other nights; there wasn't even a dust storm raging at this moment. And yet Angus 7873 was now howling, "Buddha? Buddha? Buddha?" His complaint was muffled by his suit. It was loudest and clearest inside his helmet.

Angus 7873's unpracticed howling became a pitiful yowling as his emotional state distorted the words and sounds he made. Angus 7873's arms flailed more as his stumbling became more frantic and his breathing became more spasmodic gasping and chuffing. His words now came out in pieces, "Buddh...ha,...Bu...ddha,...Buddha..."

Angus 7873 increased his pace and his footfalls took him further and faster around his ever increasing spiral, kicking up sand and dust in the otherwise still terrain. His grimace was now an outright look of terror. His eyes wet his cheeks and snot and spittle dripped from his face. Little hoses came out of his faceplate and sucked away the excess liquids only to come out again shortly afterwards to clean up more mess.

His blubbering was in full force now as Angus 7873 mumbled to Buddha and flailed about in his search. Angus 7873's data screens were now flashing alerts about his accelerated heartrate, blood flow and respiration. Angus 7873 stumbled about and became more agitated, moaning for Buddha to respond.

His suit sedated him.

The effect on Angus 7873 was immediate. Angus 7873 stopped short in his stumbling and teetered on his unsteady feet. Angus 7873's eyes fluttered as the sedative dripped into his bloodstream, according to one of his data screens. This allowed Angus 7873 to catch his breath. Angus 7873 looked around and collected himself a bit, sobbing, as his suit forced him to calm down.

The effect was external and remedial. It didn't address his real concern. Having collected himself, Angus 7873 took another tentative step forward, followed shortly by a few more and he continued his automatic spiraling search pattern. In a short time Angus 7873's face registered his anxiety again, as before, eyes popping open, mouth grimacing. Angus 7873 again called out plaintively for Buddha. "Buddha? Buddha, where are you?"

Despite the sedative Angus 7873's data screens showed how his vital signs again were climbing, a clear indicator of nothing having changed in his emotional state. As frantic as Angus 7873 was, the world around him remained as still and indifferent. Although, the night filled the area with a gloom and a dispassion that left Angus 7873 quite alone.

The tears and sobs returned in a relatively lucid moment and then Angus 7873 began running in earnest and yelling for Buddha. "BUDDHA! BUDDHA! WHERE ARE YOU? WHERE ARE YOU?" He had been anxious before, he was panicked now.

Angus 7873's feet pounded the ground as he propelled himself in his desperate search. Various data displayed on his screens as Angus 7873 chased after the elusive Buddha. "Where are you?!?"

Some of Angus 7873's data screens flashed snippets of other images or thoughts. Perhaps they were memories or maybe they were just ideas. The psychological counterpart to a television set's lost vertical hold, some of these images were of other soldiers dying on battlefields. More and more of the images were of forms of termination or a lost linkage. It was as if Angus 7873's mind was struggling to find a matching experience from the past that it could identify, analyze and synthesize. Perhaps then Angus 7873 could comprehend his current situation.

But Angus 7873 was going through a massive separation anxiety, something he had never fully experienced when he was still acknowledged by Buddha. Angus 7873 was on his own and that fact was hitting him full force, even if he didn't understand it. The implication of that fact was what was making him so anxious. He and all of the other soldiers on this planet had always been 'on their own'. But they had always felt as if they were part of something, something basic, essential and undeniable. The psychological tether had always been there, or so it seemed.

Now Angus 7873 was dealing with a simple and frightening question for the uninitiated, "What do I do now?" Given that he could barely grasp the concept of "I," he was having a very difficult time with the rest. His anxiety level was sky-rocketing as he ran around in search of Buddha. His suit again administered a sedative dosage, attempting to calm him to safer metabolic levels.

But Angus 7873 was so far gone now that it barely dampened his emotions and only allowed him to keep running, to shift gears, as it were; that being the real reason behind the sedation subroutines in the armored suits, for use in frantic battle situations, not for meditative relaxation or serenity.

Without a clear objective directly in front of Angus 7873, such as destroying an Attacker or Defender, he was just running himself ragged looking for the intangible and rather abstract Buddha. His suit administered another sedative dosage, to no avail. The array of images flashing on his data screens were now coming faster and faster, flashes of mental lightning, an electrical storm of the mind.

Hyperventilation caught up with him. Angus 7873's eyes fluttered and he stopped short. Angus 7873's head dropped forward in his helmet and his torso tilted forward as his arms hung lose. His mind swiftly gave up and let go. His legs kept him up for a moment longer, but then his whole body teetered and Angus 7873 fell forward, crashing into the sandy terrain. The cloud raised by the collapse was a fitting flourish and end to his wild hunt. The air cleared as the dust settled slowly around him.

Angus 7873 had fainted.

Angus 7873 was going to sleep, a sleep he hadn't

had in a long, long time, if ever. It was unassisted by his suit and not the result of physical damage from a battle. This sleep was due to his first real emotional breakdown. Angus 7873's eyes were slightly open despite this fact. He would sleep the sleep of a child who has suffered their first shock and has learned of the fundamental nature of their place in the universe.

His data screens gradually slowed down in their displays of information. Red alert screens gave up their demented flashing and were replaced by more nominal displays. Finally, Angus 7873's suit powered down, the lights in his helmet dimmed, as if taking a cue from the human body encased in it, and rested.

* * *

Angus 7873's half open eyes fluttered and opened wide as he returned to full consciousness. Angus 7873 grimaced and complained from pain in his neck as he lifted his head to look around. His eyes scanned the data screens as they booted up and then studied the exterior through his faceplate. The way he had fallen placed his helmet and faceplate in the sand with just the outer edges clear of obstruction. He couldn't see much of any value, it was still dark and the terrain persisted in its predawn gloominess.

Angus 7873 stirred in that spot and arched his back to get a better look. His autonomic systems established his bearings and Angus 7873 pushed himself up to his knees and then onto one leg to get a better look around. His eyes dulled a bit. The nighttime disappointed him and Angus 7873 sighed.

Angus 7873 pushed himself up further, onto both feet, and contemplated his situation. Nothing had changed, at least nothing that was helpful. "Buddha?" Angus 7873 muttered to himself. Rather than start a new irrational rampage, Angus 7873 shifted his weight and turned around, looking at his surroundings.

His face registered a dull resignation to the dark sky, the landscape and his loneliness. Angus 7873 didn't need to turn around to know what was around him. His suit provided a lot of that information automatically. But for some reason, Angus 7873 did turn and adjust his position to look around — an innately human, yet futile gesture.

Buddha was not sitting nearby waiting to help. Angus 7873 was definitively moping as he turned and gazed at the harsh and empty landscape. But one thing did catch his attention.

The horizon in one direction was lighter than the rest of it. The sky was not a uniform, star-spangled blackness. Angus 7873 looked back and forth, comparing and contrasting. Again, his data screens informed him of the particulars and all necessary information; he knew what time it was. But this was different. Seeing it for himself struck him differently.

Angus 7873 gazed at the brightening section of the horizon. With his augmented patience and mechanics, Angus 7873 just stood there and stared at the distance as it transformed. A clear line had formed between dark land and a lavender sky that bloomed from one increasingly brightening point below the horizon.

Angus 7873 adjusted his eyes and studied the stars surrounding this phenomenon. They were becoming harder to distinguish as this patch of the horizon overwhelmed them. Angus 7873 wasn't moping anymore. He had a new expression on his face. There was genuine interest, or intrigue, in his face. His anticipation was clearly evident as he stared at the horizon.

The sky, from the horizon to the meridian, had become a startling lavender color while Angus 7873 simply stood there. Angus 7873's eyes darted about as he studied the sand and rocks around him that were now clearly evident to his unaided sight. His headlamps turned off allowing him to see more naturally. The rocks and terrain hadn't really changed, but they didn't seem so harsh now.

When Angus 7873 looked back up at the sky, he was surprised to see how bright the point at the horizon had become. Warmer hues were growing from this bright point, in keeping with the reddish daytime sky of this world. Only the most resilient stars peeked through the sky now as it became more and more red.

But it was the bright meniscus at the very point where all of this had started that suddenly intrigued Angus 7873 the most. It was yellowish white compared to the ruddiness of the rest of the sky or the earlier lavender. The vividness of the colors was astonishing to Angus 7873. In fact, his jaw fell a tiny bit as he watched.

Then his face truly lit up as the meniscus on the horizon became a painfully bright source of white light. His jaw dropped open and his eyes widened as they also fought to squint against what Angus 7873 was seeing. The minutes it took for this to happen were immeasurable to Angus 7873; he was lost in the experience, and yet it seemed to occur swiftly.

The meniscus became a partial, then half, then full disc as the sun rose for a new day on this world. Angus 7873 squinted against the full strength of this sunrise. His faceplate dimmed automatically, placing a black circle over the sun, to allow his human eyes to see everything else around him. But Angus 7873 accessed the controls for that and turned it off, preferring for some reason to see this in its entirety.

This sunrise warmed him in more ways than Angus 7873 knew or could have identified. Angus 7873 stood transfixed, staring at this view. As the sun finally let go of the horizon and took on its true shape, Angus 7873 let out a tiny gasp. It was now a clear, bright disc in the new red sky, swiftly climbing to a position of dominance.

Angus 7873 finally turned away from the sun, allowing his eyes to adjust. Angus 7873 turned and studied the landscape which had changed completely. It was now a high contrast world of warming illuminated rock faces and still cold shades and shadows. But it was tangible, accessible and comprehensible. The anxiety of the night before was further away, not gone completely, but at bay. As for nighttime, it had been relegated to the edge of the opposite horizon.

Angus 7873's thoughts turned to other things for a moment as he went through a flurry of disorientation and diagnosis. But he turned back to the sunrise and stopped to watch it a while longer.

Now the sun was clearly separate from the horizon and the whole world was brightening very quickly.

Angus 7873 wouldn't have known what was making his face twitch, but it was a heightened emotional state directly related to watching this sunrise.

When the sun had finally reached two or three hand widths up from the horizon, Angus 7873 turned his attention more clearly to other matters. His data screens ran through a series of displays, offering data for his consideration. Most of this data cycled through a few times, allowing correlations with other data after his initial perusal.

Then his faceplate, not his data screens, flashed

some new information and started to plot trajectories, a series of dotted lines and labels that were locked to the terrain, no matter how he moved or shifted his position. Luminous thin lines of different colors, with tiny designators labelling them, tracked across his faceplate. These indicated the trajectories of other soldiers gone since the previous night. Angus 7873 focused on one and moved toward it.

As Angus 7873 got closer to this trajectory, it became clear that it was a set of tracks, footprints leading away from the battlefield. The night winds had softened them, but they hadn't erased them.

Angus 7873 slowly followed this track back to where it started. The source was a pit probably left by the soldier's body.

But it wasn't the pit that Angus 7873 found interesting as much as the location. It was on a gentle slope that led back down to the Tower complex where the battle had taken place. In fact, there were a lot of tracks and pits left behind in this area. Beyond this there were the last remaining salvage operations as repair crabs still scurried around with what bits and pieces of the dead and injured soldiers remained.

Angus 7873 walked around from pit to pit and track to track observing the peaceful battlefield. Something caught Angus 7873's eye. Several repair crabs were carrying a piece from a knee or elbow. Angus 7873 picked it up with most of the repair crabs hanging onto it while others dropped off onto the sand. Angus 7873 turned the piece in his huge hand. This piece of another soldier struck him as odd, as if Angus 7873 thought it should mean something more to him. But it didn't.

"Buddha?" Angus 7873 muttered again, tentatively. Angus 7873 looked up and around at the now daytime sky and the impregnable Tower complex. Angus 7873 glanced at the now painfully brilliant sun in the sky and came to some conclusion.

"Buddha? Angus reporting ninety-nine point nine, nine, nine, seven, three percent rehab and ready." Angus 7873 waited again, this time with a calmer, renewed, attitude. "Buddha? Angus reporting ninety-nine point nine, nine, nine, seven, three percent rehab. Ready. Respond."

For some reason, being ninety-nine point nine, nine, nine, seven, three percent rehabilitated wasn't good enough for Buddha. But for the last several hours since Angus 7873's diagnostic subroutine, it had clearly been good enough for him. As far as he was concerned, he was fully operational. Angus 7873 shifted his weight onto one leg and sighed. Angus 7873 blinked. Angus 7873 glanced at the tracks left by the soldiers. Gradually, ever so slowly, an idea began to occur to him.

Angus 7873 multi-tasked, transmitting the whole time, calling Buddha, while also growing this new idea in his mind. But the idea started to grow and manifest itself in his data screens, first in one, then in another, followed by a few more.

The trajectories of the departing soldiers returned to prominence on Angus 7873's faceplate. They overlaid a moire of lines over the sloping terrain of the battlefield around the Tower complex. Even in the brightness of the new day Angus 7873 could easily follow the tracks. The light of the displayed trajectories added a dappled light to Angus 7873's face that was particularly evident when he faced away from the sun. It was almost as if it were an illumination on his thought processes.

Angus 7873 noticed that there was a cluster of tracks that followed the same basic direction. Whether these had left as a group or had gone off individually wasn't immediately clear, although his faceplate indicated the real answer. A group had definitely walked off in one direction, led by one specific soldier. Perhaps it was the proximity of these tracks, or perhaps it was the grouping of these tracks, an antidote to loneliness, or perhaps it was that the tracks led off in the direction of the sunrise. Whatever it was, Angus 7873 was drawn to this information.

And so Angus 7873 began to follow them.

FOLLOWING

Angus 7873's helmet lights tracked the footprints ahead of him. "Tycho system Buddha!" Angus 7873 said in a bored voice. Angus 7873 had been following the tracks for hours, so much so that now the displayed plots on his faceplate were indicating projected trajectories that remarkably matched the actual ones left behind by the rambling soldiers.

As Angus 7873 cleared a ridge, two gorgeous planets filled the lower sky, striped by dark cirrus clouds. Angus 7873 faltered a bit as he said, "Tycho system Buddha."

"Tycho system Buddha. Respond!" Angus 7873 persisted. "Tycho system Buddha. Respond," Angus 7873 repeated. No response. Angus 7873 sighed. It was an odd sigh, a natural reaction, but it sounded artificial nonetheless, perhaps due to the force behind it or his timing.

Later, Angus 7873 reached a big, steep hill and climbed it diligently. "Tycho barada Buddha. Respond?" No response. Angus 7873's body didn't really fatigue. As long as there was a thought in his mind, his augmented body would respond and perform. Climbing this steep hill was simply a matter of time. His armored body was perfectly suited for scrabbling over this terrain. And so, Angus 7873 continued transmitting the entire time.

As soon as Angus 7873 cleared a ridge or summit, he would catch sight of dots in the distance. Angus 7873 followed them. "Tycho Buddha barada Buddha. Respond?"

Angus 7873 waited. And waited. And waited. Nothing. His data screens displayed a lot of information. One of them always showed the time as a digital counter that constantly rolled numbers. "Tycho Buddha nikto Buddha. Respond?" Angus looked at the time and watched the numbers scroll. The seconds were a blur. Minutes were slower. Hours, slower still. Days, weeks, months, and years were irrelevant to him. Angus 7873 stared at the counter and thought. He paused in his steps and stared at the year.

*　*　*

In the morning Angus 7873 was still alone and still

transmitting and still following. "Tycho Muhammad. Respond." The rising sun was glowing, limning the horizon and shifting the hue of the sky away from the nighttime blackness. Angus 7873 found himself in a rolling plain accompanied only by solitary rocks, the spray of sand that beat against him, and the sounds he made. Another day would dawn on this crabby planet as Angus followed the soldiers, step after step after step.

"Orlando forward, 42-2-11. Excellence." Angus 7873 snapped to attention and stopped in his tracks. His contact had been acknowledged. His eyes darted about scanning his numerous data screens. Angus 7873 could read the response on some of his screens. It was unclear what shocked him more: the response or his shock at the response. Angus 7873 blurted out an acknowledgement, "Copy."

"Tycho. Hold at present location," Angus 7873 added quickly. "Respond?" Angus waited and actually caught his breath.

"Copy. Holding affirmative at present location," someone responded.

Angus 7873's eyes sparkled, "Excellence." Angus 7873 didn't know exactly what he had done right to get acknowledged. Perhaps he accessed the recognition code by way of an obscure, administrative subdirectory using the Orlando directory as a proxy relay with a sublimated set of bit blocks that circumvented the usual routing subroutine. Or maybe Angus 7873 had been acknowledged before but it wasn't until now that the soldiers had transmitted an acknowledgment due to a normal delay in the server queueing and processing because of the proxy relay Angus 7873 had used. Whatever it was, Angus 7873 didn't care.

*   *   *

By the time Angus 7873 caught up to the others, the sky had turned a dull grey. His face bore an expression of almost child-like expectation as Angus 7873 trudged across the flat ground to the tiny cluster of soldiers waiting for him. The cluster grew larger as Angus 7873 got closer. "Look for the blue sky," Angus 7873 said.

"Designate," Calvin 6501 instructed. Angus 7873's data screens indicated all the names of the soldiers standing around him. There were ten of them. The data screens displayed all of them with all of their designations, vital statistics and current positions. But it was Calvin 6501 who drew most of Angus 7873's attention. Though former enemies, they now were neutral parties meeting on this deserted plain.

Likewise, Calvin 6501's data screens indicated a schematic of Angus 7873, but no identification, no designation — name or numbers, friend or foe. It was as though Angus 7873 didn't exist. As far as Calvin 6501 and the rest of the waiting soldiers were concerned, Angus

7873 was simply an outlined soldier standing in front of them, operational and real, but anonymous. All of his information, current location, etc., was displayed, but not his name. In short, only what the soldiers could perceive showed up on their data screens. Angus 7873 hit on the right communication protocol for Calvin 6501 or any of them to hear him and react. Otherwise, Angus 7873 was a blank.

"Angus. 7873," Angus 7873 responded to Calvin 6501 and the rest. A cursor scrolled down directories as Calvin 6501 called up that number on his screens. However, what showed up was: `No contact: KIA (Killed In Action)`.

"Angus, 7873 has been destroyed. Killed in Action," Calvin 6501 said. According to their information, Angus 7873 was dead and gone. His vital statistics jumped as his blood pressure rose with his anxiety. Angus 7873 became more frantic. Angus 7873 could see what they were seeing. Angus 7873 could receive their logistical and autonomic communications. They just couldn't receive his.

"Negative. Angus seven eight, sev..." Angus 7873 said, trailing off. Angus 7873 watched them in confusion, his ID number, 7873, clearly labeled on his armor along with his name. Angus 7873 shifted his weight and tried to speak again, to formulate the appropriate response or explanation.

"BEEEOOOP," an alarm went off in all of their suits. "Rest period," Calvin 6501 said, as the de facto commanding officer of the small group. All of the soldiers sat down while Angus 7873 remained standing and stared at them. They, however, ignored him. Angus 7873 walked around them, studying them. They had all switched to Rest Mode. Except for Angus 7873, all of their suit lights had dimmed to half power. Angus 7873 looked at his data screens and found his own gauges for Primary Power that seemed to indicate a need for replenishment of some sort. It was a color coded gauge and his levels were in the red reserves as opposed to the more comforting green zone.

Angus 7873 studied the pale faces of the resting soldiers. Some of their eyelids fluttered as Angus 7873 stared at them. Angus 7873 got very to close to them, scrutinizing their faces. Their skin looked sallow and dry, peeling in some areas. Despite their helmets' sun protections, they were vulnerable to sunburns and the aging effects of sunlight. That is why these soldiers all looked older than their respective ages, which ranged from mid-twenties to late forties. Angus 7873 stopped at one of the soldiers and stared at her, Monica 2488. Her eyes were almost shut and her lips moved silently. Angus 7873 could see her eyeballs moving beneath the lids.

Suddenly, her faceplate became opaque hiding her from sight. Angus 7873 looked at the others and their faceplates had gone opaque as well. Then, the same images started playing on all of their faceplates, as if these were personal movie screens. Angus 7873 was basically watching these movies from behind the movie screen, the reverse of what the soldiers were seeing. They watched happy images of people running through fields of grass in a beautiful world with a blue sky. Angus 7873 watched as if he had never seen this before. In a way, Angus 7873 hadn't. Things Angus 7873 didn't recognize populated these images: a dog playing with people, birds flying in the sky, flowers, trees, not to mention the grass and the blue sky. Angus 7873 looked around at all of the soldiers sitting in a cluster with these brilliant images flashing on their faceplates.

Angus 7873 stood up straight and thought about it. Rest Mode; Angus 7873 didn't get it. Angus 7873 looked at the dirty sky; it wasn't that artificial blue in the flashing images. Angus 7873 looked at his data screen that flashed the words Rest Mode and selected that item. His faceplate immediately went opaque and started displaying the same video, in progress, synchronized with the rest.

Angus 7873 was suddenly confronted by the sound accompanying the images of men and women and smaller versions (children) running around and laughing. The laughter sounded so strange to him. His face twitched involuntarily in reaction to the laughter and the images of these figures running after each other. A voice filled his helmet, "Clean air, green grass, blue skies. This is what life is all about. A place that you can call home, where you can raise your family in joy and comfort. That is what it's all about. That is why you're doing what you're doing...and we are thankful."

The video ended and Angus 7873 reared back as if assaulted by the images in his helmet. Angus 7873 looked at the soldiers whose faceplates had cleared and studied them. Their eyes were open but still dazed looking, sleepy. None of them seemed affected by what they had just seen. Finally, Angus 7873 sat down next to Monica 2488.

The suits started making a small odd noise. Angus 7873 looked around for the source of this new noise. Angus 7873 looked at his data screens and referred to what the rest of the soldiers were doing. According to the current data selection on Monica 2488's screen, her suit was feeding her, same as the others. Angus 7873 looked at his own status. His suit was not feeding him. Angus 7873 stared at the soldiers and then looked at his own suit, thinking. Angus 7873 scrolled through his data screens.

"This guy walks into a bar," Monica 2488 spoke suddenly. Angus 7873 looked at her, startled and confused. "He tells the bartender, 'Pissfuckshit.' Laughs and laughs. 'I bet him five hundred dollars,' " she said. Just as suddenly, the rest of the soldiers laughed mechanically. Angus 7873 stared at Monica 2488, wondering what he had just seen.

"This woman walks into a bar. Guy says 'What are you doing with that pig.' She says, 'Okay where's that bear.' The dog." Apparently, it had been Calvin 6501's turn. Angus 7873 stared intently at Calvin 6501, who now was quiet. Again the soldiers laughed, as if programmed to laugh. Eustus 2190 then told one, "Three whores were talking to each other. 'I'll grant you three wishes. Paint my house.' "

The soldiers laughed again. Angus 7873 stared at them. Angus 7873 then studied his data screens and scrolled down a menu. Angus 7873 found: `Food` · · · · · · · · · · · · · · `FGST 8766584`. Angus 7873 punched in the numerical combination using his keypad hand and his suit began dispensing nutrients into his bloodstream, according to the screens.

"City folk stop at a farm. Farmer says they stop to talk to him," Garth 5312 said. Angus 7873's suit was now making the same sound as the others. Angus 7873 looked at Garth 5312 as he continued, "There's a pig in a pen. 'Why's that pig got three wooden legs?' 'You don't eat a pig saves the house.' " More canned laughter followed his recitation. Angus 7873 was lost.

Angus 7873 looked at his data screens and noticed a blinking selection: `REST MODE/DIVERSION/`. Angus 7873 selected it and found he had accessed the jokes file. Leni 2221, a female, told another joke. "Two policemen stop a horse. The horse tells them to take a hike. Don't know what to do with it. Makes a million in the stock market. Two to turn the horse, one to write the report." More pre-programmed laughter filled the air. Angus 7873 had the same jokes on file and read along: `"Two to turn the horse, one to write the report. GotoCode^X2377 ^Laughter^ 86 **"`

Angus 7873 stared out at them. They laughed and then stopped abruptly. Another joke appeared on Angus 7873's screen: `"A man picks up his mother-in-law. His wife needs a face lift. Everytime she kisses her on the cheek. Happy."`

No one said it out loud. It blinked insistently at Angus 7873 unlike the other jokes did. Angus 7873 studied the others and wondered. The joke stopped blinking on-screen and switched to the GotoCode and all of the soldiers laughed mechanically again, startling Angus 7873.

They were laughing at "his" joke.

The rusty sky darkened around them, turning bluer as the stars began to peek through again. Another soldier told another pseudo-joke that had come on-screen. Again they laughed. Stopped. On and on. Angus 7873 looked up at the darkening sky and muttered, "...look for the blue sky."

Their pseudo-jokes drifted into the darkening night

sky and floated up to space as aimless radio noise. An orbiting satellite heard the jokes as it watched over the dirt planet and the crescent of day waned in the expanse of blackness.

*   *   *

A teenager stood, wearing a grey jumpsuit with tubes and wires attached to it. Machines patched wires to his head. Laser scan-lines flashed across his face. "...look for the blue sky," Angus 7873's disembodied voice said. A robotic arm swung over him. It too could speak, in raspy, metallic tones, "Look for the blue sky." The anxious teenager responded, "Look for the blue sky." Other robotic machinery moved into action as the young Angus 7873 was hoisted and placed on a work table. Arms moved pieces of armor into place and started building the armored spacesuit he would live in for the rest of his existence. All the heavy machines moving about scared him. He stared at all of it, his eyes flitting from thing to another. His voice was rising with his level of anxiety. "Look for the blue sky!" he repeated.

Auto-welders soldered sections together. Probes tested motors and systems in the suit. "Look for the blue sky, look for the blue sky, look for the blue sky, look for the blue sky!" he said, frantically. "Look for the blue sky," the robotic arm repeated, as if acknowledging a mantra or a blessing.

In no time Angus was encased in his shiny new armor as the robots installed the collar section and finished it all off by placing his helmet on him. "LOOK FOR THE BLUE —" his voice muffled as the seal closed him in. He was part of a long assembly line consisting of more work tables and more young humans all of whom were being encased in their individual armored suits. These images dissolved as Angus 7873's screamed mantra faded inside his helmet to be replaced by memories that were so old that they didn't really belong to Angus 7873.

A man. A woman. Her naked back. The touch. The feel of her skin. His hand on the small of her back. The warmth....

Angus 7873 had never experienced that sensation, but somehow he knew how it felt.

THINKING

Angus 7873 slept with his head hung forward in his helmet. Angus 7873 had drooled a little bit. The sun was rising on the horizon and sweat had formed a sheen on his skin.

Angus 7873 opened his eyes abruptly.

The rest of the soldiers were standing around him, towering over him. Apparently Rest Mode was over. But they weren't paying attention to him in the least. Angus 7873 watched them as they instinctively shifted around and headed out in one direction, trudging in their oddly smooth yet mechanical way across the terrain. Clearly, Angus 7873 couldn't hear what they were hearing. Angus 7873 got up, shook his head, looked around when an idea occurred to him.

Angus 7873 looked back at their little camp, checking to see if they had left anything behind. The only thing left behind was a semicircle of impressions in the sand made by their huge armored bodies at rest.

The morning was clear, facilitating Angus 7873 in quickly catching up to the traveling soldiers. The light that fell on them was particularly red as the sun rose in the sky. While the soldiers were single-minded in their locomotion, Angus 7873 was still shaking off his sleep. It showed in his movements as Angus 7873 faltered periodically, stumbling on the uneven terrain.

The soldiers walked along a scar left by an ancient river with Angus 7873 following them from a short distance behind. They moved practically in unison. While they weren't in lock-step, they were all moving at the same pace, as one unit. They were circling around a butte ahead of them, rather than climbing it. As they came around the butte, Angus 7873 saw another shape on the horizon ahead of them. It was huge, not as huge as the butte they were circumventing, but big. It seemed ancient, mostly buried under years of blown sand. It was artificial, not a geological structure, and it clearly was not human.

It was a derelict ship and the soldiers ignored it.

But Angus 7873 stared at it. Looking back and forth between the alien ship and the wandering soldiers, Angus

7873 wandered away from them and approached it. It was bulbous, organic-looking, like a big bug, a hornet, something with black and yellow bands and rounded shapes and sections. Angus 7873 scanned it:

◇◇

```
    <.]] .,>>,// ^   ^(   %#3 @3*448970 [
]669)00 IRON\|| ^   ^(   %#3@3*DEUTERIUM
    448970 [ vivv]669)00 ] ,// | \||
      ^   ^(   %#3 @3*,// | \|^CARBON
GRAPHITE^( %#3 @3*448,// | \|| ^ ^%#3
@3*4489MAGNESIUM70 [ ]669)00 ] 970 [
 m ]6PHOSPHATE69)00 ] ,// | \|| ^   ^(
  %#3 v v@3*448SILICA-SUBSTRATES970 [
    ]669)00]42424448970 [ ]669)00
```

◇◇

Long antennae curved out from it, some broken, snapped back by the crash that took place so long ago. It was buried halfway into the riverbed. Angus 7873 walked up to it and touched it tentatively. Despite his high-powered sensors and his ability to collect so much data about anything in his presence, Angus 7873 felt compelled to touch it, almost as a final confirmation of its existence. Angus 7873 walked along, sliding his hand on the hull until he found a crew member.

Petrified at a portal was a traveler as ancient as the ship, mostly encased in a spacesuit of their design. It seemed pensive, leaning against the frame. Angus 7873 studied it. The crew member also wore armor. Angus 7873 turned to look at his companions but they had gone on. "Calvin 6501? Monica 2488? Wait for Angus," Angus

7873 said. Nothing; they did not respond.

Angus 7873 searched for the right protocol that the others would obey. "Tycho Muhammad. Stop." Up river, they stopped. Angus 7873 listened for a response. "Who stopped us?" Eustus 2190 asked absently.

"Angus," Angus 7873 answered.

"Angus what?" Eustus 2190 asked. Angus 7873 looked for an answer. "Angus found...something," Angus 7873 ventured.

"What?" Calvin 6501 asked.

"Insufficient data," Angus 7873 said. "Wait," Angus 7873 added after a moment. Angus 7873 listened. Nothing. "Evidence of crashed transport..." Angus 7873 added.

"Crashed transport of what origin?" Calvin 6501 asked.

"Unclear," Angus 7873 answered. Angus 7873 looked ahead, shined his helmet lights into the portal and entered. It was dark inside, sand-filled, cramped. Angus 7873 could barely squeeze into the space.

Angus 7873 found a handle and tried it; no go. Angus 7873 tried harder. The handle broke. Angus 7873 looked at the broken handle in his big augmented hand.

"Moving," Calvin 6501 announced.

"What? No, wait," Angus 7873 said. Angus 7873 looked around the chamber. Angus 7873 had to go. Angus 7873 studied the broken handle in his huge hand and then let it drop.

Angus 7873 gave a final look at the entire chamber,

from one side to the other, as if trying to absorb its meaning and any answers it held for later reference. Angus 7873 exited the portal and hurried after his companions, frequently looking back at the derelict ship.

It was more difficult to walk while looking back over his shoulder, so Angus 7873 finally gave up and turned his attention forward. But the discovery had shocked him so much and in such a new way that Angus 7873 couldn't stop thinking about it. As soon as the soldiers saw Angus 7873 approaching them, they turned and continued walking. Angus 7873 strained to catch up and after a while he did.

"Calvin. It was a ship," Angus 7873 tried to impress upon him. But Calvin 6501 ignored him. Angus 7873 stared at him and looked around. "Calvin 6501. Calvin 6501," Angus 7873 added trying to impress on him the impact of his find. But Calvin 6501 had one thought in his mind: to continue walking forward, wherever it was they were going.

A thought popped into Angus 7873's head. "Where are we going?" Angus 7873 asked. Calvin 6501 stammered for an answer. As if surprised by a recollection or suddenly opening a computer file with the correct answer plainly spelled out, Calvin 6501 responded, "Forward. Secure and hold for PetroCom! Look for the blue sky." Angus 7873 cocked his head, uncertainly...

"Affirmative," Angus 7873 said, at a loss for anything

better to say. Angus 7873 followed quietly. Angus 7873 looked back at the wreckage they had sidestepped, not quite with an expression of longing, but his thoughts definitely preoccupied by it.

*   *   *

After much walking, the dry river bed had transformed into an alluvial ridge on which the soldiers were travelling. Later still, the soldiers crossed the basin of an old volcano. The soldiers cut a line across the old caldera that eventually led them out and down the other side of the volcano to the valley below.

The far side of the valley was the mouth of a canyon. The soldiers trudged across the valley and headed directly to the canyon. There, the soldiers arrived at another Tower complex. This one sat idly by as the other had, with only the minimum of apparent activity, the most obvious being spotlights on automatic operation.

Sunlight sliced through muddy clouds. Patterns played on the Tower and its helical support structures. The soldiers sat down to wait within view of the Tower. Angus 7873 walked around the soldiers. After so much walking Angus 7873 wasn't ready to sit down. Angus 7873 circled around them in mild fascination at their behavior. However, they simply ignored him as they waited. Angus 7873 noticed that their data screens were displaying a new message now. Angus 7873 leaned closer and saw that Calvin 6501's data screen displayed their current mode:

◇◇◇

```
    WAITING FOR SUPPLEMENTAL TROOPS;
    HRS:58:27:30; PLANT DEFENSE: 60;
  ATTACKERS: 60; **INSUFFICIENT TROOPS
   TO START BATTLE!; 20% SUPERIORITY
       REQUIRED TO START BATTLE!
```

◇◇◇

Angus 7873 searched his own data screens and quickly pulled up the same information to review it. For some reason, even though Angus 7873 apparently had the same information as the other soldiers, it wasn't displaying automatically as it did for them.

Angus 7873 watched Calvin 6501 as he looked at his data screens, one after the other, left, bottom left, bottom right, right, top, left, bottom left, bottom right, right, top, left, bottom left...and so on. Angus 7873 didn't know what to make of Calvin 6501's mechanical quality. But then they were all like that. Even Angus 7873. In fact, Angus 7873 stood still and watched them for hours as they waited. As much as Angus 7873 stared in wonder he hadn't yet realized that he didn't know what they were waiting for. The single difference was that while they seemed content with the information on their screens, Angus 7873 was just a bit more curious, wanting a little more.

A steady parade of clouds, drizzle, mud and sunlight

passed by them as they waited, followed by more clouds, wind and sand. A similarly even and uneven progression of facial movements, blinking and tics passed over Angus 7873's face as time went by. Sometime around the late afternoon, a noteworthy thing happened to Angus 7873: he gave a deep long sigh. Later, at some point, night came to visit.

Helmet lights came on. Sand had piled up on their helmets and shoulders while they had been waiting, demonstrating how patient they could be.

Along with curiosity came boredom. Angus 7873 watched. His eyelids drooped. *His hand on the small of her back....* His eyelids fluttered. Opened wide, interested; lights were cresting a hill in the distance, pinpricks.

Gradually, more appeared; three, then eight, then twelve, eighteen, twenty-one pairs of helmet lights.

Inside Calvin 6501's helmet an alarm went off: BWOO-OMP; BWOO-OMP; BWOO-OMP. His data screen began flashing:

```
PROXIMITY ALERT!  PROXIMITY ALERT!⅂
   POSSIBLE SUPPLEMENTAL ATTACKERS!
#<⅂<>> ^  ƂƂ^^^^ ^^^ ^^_=|\\°⅂ PEACE
   CODE ^Ƨ2/*Ƃ⅂ FRIENDLY CONFIRMED⅂
   SUPPLEMENTAL ATTACKERS:**2⅃⅂ 35%
             SUPERIORITY.
```

His cursor blinked expectantly. Angus 7873

accessed the same data. With the arrival of these other soldiers the whole collective had now become a new group of Attackers.

Calvin 6501 looked out at the approaching helmet lights. "This blue sky brought to you by GCS," he said.

All of the Attackers heard a chime in their helmets and then joined in chorus, "This blue sky brought to you by GCS." The soldiers stood up and started to fan out, flanking the Tower.

"Tycho Muhammad. Flank Furlong Midway Vectors twenty-seven, thirty-two, forty-six, fifty-five. Mark," Calvin 6501 ordered.

"Mark vectors," an Attacker responded over their commlink.

"Good, roger. No sign of detection," Calvin 6501 added.

"True here," the Attacker responded.

Angus 7873 tried to keep up with the sudden developments. Unlike the others, who seemed directed in their actions, Angus 7873 was not included in their games. The new Attackers took up positions according to Calvin 6501's information, a rough semicircle around the Tower. Helmet lights dotted the terrain. Angus 7873 wasn't sure what to do. Angus 7873 watched nervously and tentatively took a similar position.

"Attacker line. Ready," Monica 2488 said, off somewhere. BOO-WOP; another acknowledgement code sounded. "ATTACK," she added. Angus 7873 was surprised. Angus 7873 looked around and then referred to his data screens: NEUTRAL MODE!

Angus 7873 checked the other Attackers' codes that he was receiving and could see the difference: ATTACK MODE! Angus 7873 scrolled down the options: NEUTRAL, ATTACK, DEFEND. Angus 7873 looked around and hesitated. Except for one set of helmet lights, Angus 7873, the various helmet lights closed in on the Tower.

Angus 7873 watched them advance on the Tower. Monica 2488 was the first. She launched a rocket. Then a spray of lasers lit up the night.

Angus 7873 accessed his Mode menu. Angus 7873 scrolled down and changed his NEUTRAL to ATTACK.

Angus 7873 followed them into battle. Angus 7873 aimed his laser cannon and fired. The laser sliced through the air, hit the Tower and left a bubbling black streak on the surface. It was a largely ineffectual shot but it was noteworthy in as much as Angus 7873 had fully intended it, based entirely on his own thoughts. This perhaps had been the first time that Angus 7873 had ever done something of his own volition, at least in a long, long time.

All the Attackers were now firing, launching grenades and rockets, advancing on the objective.

Light sliced out and spread into a fan from the Tower as its huge doors opened revealing the Defenders in silhouette. Helmet lights came on and the Defenders came out — FIRING! Lasers, grenades and rockets traced out from the Tower's entry.

Attackers were hit. Arms. Legs. Heads. Leni 2221 raised her cannon to fire and was hit by a laser. Her shoulder plate shattered, spinning her around from the impact, causing her to fall.

Garth 5312 pumped his grenade launcher, fired a grenade. He pumped again, fired another grenade.

The grenades landed near the Tower and sunk into the sand, in front of the Defenders. The first one exploded, throwing two Defenders back. The second one exploded. Three more Defenders were blown back.

Leni 2221 stood up. She aimed carefully. A laser hit a Defender's leg and blasted his knee away. Leni fired, boring through a Defender's helmet. The Defender dropped, face down. Another Defender approached her.

Leni shot at the power pack on the downed Defender. The power pack exploded, knocking the second Defender off his feet. The Defender jumped back on his feet and returned fire, launching a grenade.

That grenade hit Leni 2221 square and stuck in her armor. Five. Four. Three. Two.

One. Leni 2221 exploded. Her head and appendages blew in five directions. Torso blasted apart. Leni 2221's helmet knocked another Attacker down.

Five Defenders formed a line, walking and firing lasers, slicing across at head level.

Angus 7873 ducked and shot back. Angus 7873 knocked one Defender down.

Angus 7873 pumped and launched a grenade. It exploded without hitting any Defenders. Angus 7873 fired again.

The soldiers were no longer in concentric semicircles. Attackers and Defenders were mixing in the battle and fire crisscrossed between them, creating a melee.

Angus 7873 fired again and killed a Defender. Three laser beams, crossfire from the melee, trapped Angus 7873 in a triangle for a split second. Angus 7873 turned and cut down another Defender with his laser cannon.

Explosion. It knocked Angus 7873 down. He pushed himself up, looking around. Soldiers were everywhere. Flashes, explosions. The nighttime battle lit up the whole canyon.

A Defender spotted Angus 7873. He walked up to him, aimed and exploded. Angus 7873 raised his arms against the shrapnel and debris raining on him; Defender parts, pieces, everywhere.

Angus 7873 got up. "All Attackers. Laser strafe on three," Calvin 6501 ordered. BEEP. BEEP. BEEP. The Attackers ducked. Calvin 6501 swung his laser beam across the battlefield hitting several Defenders, knocking some down and slicing through others. Angus 7873 watched Calvin 6501's beam sweep across the battlefield, toward him, knocking down Defenders. Angus 7873's slow reaction caused him to barely duck in time to avoid Calvin 6501's laser beam.

The Attackers shot at the remaining Defenders, having achieved a clear advantage. The Attackers approached the Tower and downed more Defenders. They were now immediately surrounding the Tower.

Eustus 2190 exploded, knocking Angus 7873 down. A particle beam had struck from above and destroyed Eustus 2190. Unlike the focused light of lasers a particle beam consisted of accelerated energy particles that had a more solid nature than lasers. Lasers were scalpels, particle beams were hatchets. Angus 7873 looked up to see that Eustus 2190's lower half was still standing. Fire burned where the torso had been. Then the knees bent and the legs slowly fell over.

Beams dropped all over. Particle beams. Slicing. Punching. Eliminating Attackers, killing quickly.

Angus 7873 crawled forward. Strunz 3197 was hit, his left arm removed by a beam. Angus 7873 looked at Strunz 3197 as he screamed and tumbled to the ground. Angus 7873 crawled over to him. "Strunz! Strunz!" Angus 7873 protested.

Strunz 3197 rolled over, struggled to his feet and picked up his laser cannon with his other arm. He resumed firing.

Angus 7873 stared at Strunz 3197's severed stump. Repair crabs had appeared instantly and stanched the bleeding. A section of the armor closed, like a camera iris, sealing what was left of his arm. The crabs further patched it up and then they disappeared, some scurrying to the nooks and cubbyholes of Strunz 3197's suit while others scuttled off entirely.

Angus 7873 looked into the sky and saw the Flying Vehicle that hounded them in the last battle. Helping the Defenders, it continued to harry the Attackers as it fired another beam, a direct hit, on Strunz 3197 and destroyed him. Angus 7873 gasped, "Strunz!"

Angus 7873 continued crawling. The weapons fire ignored him as Angus 7873 found himself on a path to the Tower, just twenty meters from the door. Angus 7873 got to his feet.

The Flying Vehicle boldly hovered meters above the battle, picking off soldiers. It evaded shrapnel and debris from the resulting explosions effortlessly, as if completely aware of its surroundings.

More Attackers dropped as the balance shifted. Angus 7873 saw a Defender fire on an Attacker, Gorman 1180. A finely tuned beam poked through his neck, making him splutter strange words, "slakd reererewqd ew erwq rewq rewq rq rew rqw rewq rq reqw rwqrewr..." Gorman 1180 fell backwards.

Angus 7873 noticed that the Tower doors were open directly in front of him. Pausing, he surveyed the battle. Attackers were falling everywhere. Defenders were making a minimal effort and yet the advantage had been lost.

Angus 7873 looked up at the Flying Vehicle. It was practically sitting there, the king of the hill, the master of its manor. And then something new happened to Angus 7873. He got angry.

Angus 7873 aimed, fired his laser and hit the Flying Vehicle square in the middle, hitting armor. It dodged to the left, as if surprised, and instantly retaliated. But it targeted and hit a Defender, instead of Angus 7873 who was standing too close to the Defender. He fell as Angus 7873 watched, knocked out of commission. The Flying Vehicle seemed to double take, thinking twice about its split-second reaction.

Seeing the doors to the Tower standing open in front of him, Angus 7873 walked toward them. He was nervous, expecting to get hit at any moment; this was the closest anyone had ever got to breaching a Tower perimeter. Ten meters, five meters, at the doors. Angus 7873 walked through the air-lock system and the outer doors closed, allowing the inner doors to slide open automatically.

The inside of the Tower was like a white hangar, with heavy reinforcing beams, industrial markings, service robots casually going about their business. A data screen in Angus 7873's helmet suddenly showed the layout of the Tower, which surprised him. Even

Angus 7873 knew this should be classified information. The pertinence of this information was somehow delicious. Angus 7873 stared at the surroundings, for a moment forgetting the urgency of the battle outside.

Angus 7873 studied his data screen and the options now listed there:

```
Communication/Telemetry.
Cooling.
Ground level.
Maintenance.
Mining.
Reactor.
Refinery.
Repair.
Power.
```

The last item drew his attention: POWER. Another one of his data screens displayed a list of strategies and tactics: OPTIMAL TARGET POINTS / Primary - Power pack.

Angus 7873 thought. Angus 7873 looked at the layout of the Tower and made an inquiry. His thoughts were instantly patched into his suit's computers, part of the hybridizing between human and machine. INQUIRY: next course of action? Angus 7873 waited.

"Default attack mode," his suit responded. **Power** Angus 7873 stared at the screen: Default Optimal target: **Power**

His data screen immediately displayed a schematic of

the ground floor leading to the Power sector. A homing beacon assisted him as well, a hotter/colder direction system. It was all very simple and Angus 7873 knew how to follow directions well. So, Angus 7873 started walking.

Angus 7873 reached a corkscrew ramp and descended two levels to the subterranean area. Angus 7873 approached the Power plant area and found the reactor, the whole time following the map on his data screen and the homing beacon that beeped faster the closer he moved to the objective.

As Angus 7873 reached his objective, one data screen in particular gave him new and obvious information:

```
               WARNING!
        AVOID REACTOR SPACE!
  (Weapons prohibited in reactor area.
Sec.846611.47. Possible reactor damage
               due to...)
```

Nonetheless, Angus 7873 faced the reactor. Another data screen gave him tactical information. As odd, as unusual as this situation was, Angus 7873 was still a soldier with a specific agenda and his many supporting subroutines dictated clear actions to take in a given situation. While his strategy may have been unclear, his tactics were very clear:

Angus 7873 entered a large cylindrical area where a huge dynamo sat in the middle. Lights started spinning. Alarms went off. Angus 7873 scanned the area before proceeding.

A schematic in Angus 7873's helmet highlighted the target. Angus 7873 made an adjustment to his cannon. Angus 7873 stared at the massive dynamo that powered the reactor's maintenance system and then launched a grenade. With a 'chunk' it stuck into the dynamo's outer casing. Angus 7873 launched a second grenade. Chunk. It stuck also. Digital counters on the grenades immediately started counting.

Angus 7873 turned and left the dynamo, moving quicker than before, innately aware of the urgency of the situation. Placing two grenades around a dynamo that was connected to a nuclear reactor in a Tower complex could create a series of explosions that would culminate in a meltdown, a nuclear reaction that would turn the complex into a huge crater. Angus 7873 could hear an audio countdown in his helmet from the grenades as he ascended to the ground level.

Maintenance crabs came out to look. The first one to a grenade was clearly surprised. Immediately, the word went out and the crabs went into a frenzy as they scurried around the grenades, tapping, testing, probing and prodding them. In an instant the dynamo area became host to a swarm of repair crabs as they all responded to word of the two grenades.

Angus 7873 cleared the ramp as other crabs streamed past him to the lower levels and swung his cannon around, just in case. The area was clear. No one had responded to his breach. Angus 7873 moved toward the doors. Instead, Defenders were outside, aiming away from him.

Angus 7873 reached the doors, passed through the air-lock and stood in the center of the open outer doorway. Three Defenders' backs were immediately in front of him. Angus 7873 aimed and started on the left. He fired his laser. Bull's eye! Middle. Bull's eye! Right. Bull's eye! But that was easy since they were ignoring him, looking the other way without him registering on their screens. Angus 7873 continued forward, shooting, clearing a path for his urgent exit from the Tower.

"Attackers! Fire in the hole!" Angus 7873 announced according to protocol. He was only referring to the grenades he had just deposited in the reactor area.

Some of the crabs managed to dislodge one grenade from the dynamo and frantically scurried to dispose of it. There was dissension among them on how to dispose of it. Some clearly wanted to dismantle it. Others wanted to get it out of the Power Sector entirely. Despite their lack of solidarity, they managed to split it open as the digital counter reached...ZERO. They paused, expecting it to explode. It didn't.

Then the other grenade exploded. The dynamo casing ruptured and collapsed to one side. The dynamo then exploded in multiple stages of ever-increasing blasts. The repair crabs that had collected around the grenades were thrown across the area. All the lights flickered in the Power plant area, indeed the entire Tower complex, and then went out.

Just outside the Tower, Angus 7873 was buffeted by the shockwaves from the explosions. Angus 7873 steadied himself.

The Flying Vehicle pitched. The external Tower lights went out causing emergency lights illuminate. The Flying Vehicle recovered after a momentary loss of altitude, as if it had been distracted by the new developments.

The remaining Defenders gave up and turned to take refuge in the Tower. It was no longer time for battle, it was repair time for all of them and the Tower, as their data screens now indicated.

But Angus 7873 turned and fired at the retreating Defenders who passed him. Angus 7873 struck two. Three. But the rest of the Attackers stopped shooting and simply stood by. Angus 7873 noticed them with confusion.

Inside the Tower complex, pressure and heat gauges

quickly dropped and rose respectively. Computer screens displayed new frantic alerts:

```
EMERGENCY EMERGENCY EMERGENCY
     **FULL GENERATOR FAILURE**
  **REACTOR COOLANT POWER FAILURE**

 **REACTOR COOLANT PRESSURE LOSS**
DANGER DANGER DANGER DANGER DANGER
```

Sirens wailed. Red lights spun. Klaxons. Codes.

Angus 7873 had the same message on one of his data screens. Angus 7873 suddenly realized what it meant as he did a double-take and frantically warned, "All Attackers,... evacuate field!"

Monica 2488's data screens indicated the current situation as well:

```
        **REACTOR EMERGENCY!
   **EVACUATE ALL NON-ESSENTIAL
             PERSONNEL!
            correction
        **REACTOR EMERGENCY!
    **EVACUATE ALL PERSONNEL!
         **REACTOR FAILURE!
```

Monica 2488 stared at the screen, not knowing what it meant.

"All Attackers, evacuate field! The reactor is going to detonate!" Angus 7873 warned in more detail. She didn't get it. Instead she looked up. All of the Tower's emergency lights were flashing. Angus 7873 ran toward her. "Tycho Muhammad. Calvin 6501?" she transmitted. "Confirm situation analysis," she asked him.

"Stand by, Monica 2488," Calvin 6501 said. Calvin 6501 didn't get it either.

"Evacuate field. Reactor emergency," Angus 7873 urged. "All Attackers, evacuate field. The reactor is going to detonate!" Angus 7873 passed them, running away from the Tower. Monica 2488 was persuaded by dint of his exuberant example.

"Code nine, nine, nine! Emergency. Reactor. Failure. Evacuate coordinates three-seven-three, six, oh-oh, eighteen-two-two and nine-five-one. Mark," she suddenly transmitted a more precise warning as she now seemed to understand. Monica 2488 turned to flee. Calvin 6501 hesitated. Some Attackers started to turn away from the Tower as well, but others hesitated. Unsure.

About half of the remaining Attackers were now fleeing. Calvin 6501 turned to follow them. Stopped. Turned back. Stopped. Turned again. Confused. Finally, he ran after them.

Huge armor moved quickly. These suits were designed for the heat of battle and the required agility. Therefore they climbed a ridge leading out of the canyon. The other Attackers, finally understanding the urgency of the situation, turned and fled from the battleground.

Inside the Tower heat gauges indicated rapidly rising temperatures. Pressure gauge indications dropped equally fast.

The Flying Vehicle fired on the retreating Attackers. Then it stopped shooting. Something told it to reconsider its actions. It throttled up drastically, causing its engines to whine in complaint, and shot across the landscape in a straight line away from the Tower. Some of the Defenders — very few — tried to flee.

Inside the Tower heat and pressure gauges passed their redlines and finally hit their limits.

Angus 7873 was with Monica 2488 out in front of the fleeing soldiers. Calvin 6501 was close behind with the other Attackers.

The ridge crest was in sight.

Thirty meters.

Twenty.

Ten.

Over it. Angus stumbled.

Fell. Rolled down the slope.

Calvin 6501 cleared it. The others followed clumsily.

The last Attackers and Defenders ran in the dark night as fast as they could, nearing the ridge.

The Tower was now a

WHITE FLASH.

The reactor exploded. The blast incinerated everything within sight of the canyon mouth. The last few Attackers and Defenders too slow to understand the situation were vaporized in mid-step on the hot side of the ridge.

Those who reached the shielded side of the ridge were saved from the heat.

The shockwave lifted the fleeing Attackers and Defenders and hurled them in a wave of molten sand. Some were dismembered by the force. Others were smashed like empty cans.

Angus 7873, Monica 2488 and Calvin 6501 were thrown like toys. They tumbled and rolled to painful stops at the bottom of the ridge — *His hand on the small of her back...* — The wind hurled by the shockwave buried them under tons of sand and debris.

A roiling mushroom cloud surged into the sky from the center of the canyon mouth where the Tower stood. It illuminated the area for some time, then it gradually dimmed. Darkness covered the battleground and Angus 7873 was buried.

ANGUS

Smoke continued to billow from ground zero the following day. A huge black-stained crater remained where the Tower had been. Everything in the immediate blast area looked like it was smoldering, despite a cold wind blowing sand across the former battlefield. As for the Tower complex, it had vanished — completely vaporized.

The day was bright and oddly hopeful. The sunlight shone with a crisp clarity that it imparted to everything in the vicinity. As the sun rose in the rusty sky, the sand particles sparkled like tiny balls of glass. The sand dunes had been combed by the wind overnight and all of the buried soldiers were just slightly larger dunes scattered throughout the area. The only disruption to this was the evidence of thousands of tiny tracks from these dunes left by repair crabs that had done their work and larger tracks left by repaired soldiers that had gone back online. But the wind was slowly erasing this evidence as well.

An audio signal sounded nearby: HOO, TIK. HOO, TIK.

Angus was unconscious, his helmet was fogged with condensation. His eyes flitted under his eyelids. His head hung on his neck in his dark helmet. His data screens fluttered on sequentially, illuminating his face. They alternately flashed on and off as his suit's system assessed internal and external conditions and gathered its wits. The screens cleared up and displayed the following:

```
Repair sub-program.doc.889.347174 end
          DAMAGE INVENTORY
     An error occurred in diagnostic
    procedure. All systems are working
     except ENET-1 microprocessor, from
             previous damage.
Telemetry broken. Malfunction in ENET-1
            microprocessor.
```

The display ended with another sound cue. His glass faceplate was just a fogged and sand-obstructed rust color with legs of condensation trailing down. The only light in the helmet came from his screens, or so it seemed.

The rest of his screens listed information and

variables related to his life signs, internal and external temperatures and analyses of the vicinity. His suit continued the process of waking up the Colonial Militant, so Angus opened his eyes slowly. He blinked a few times, squinted and then looked around the inside of his fogged helmet. His limbs pushed and pulled, shifting his position in the sand. He lifted his head to get a better look through his faceplate. He stared in confusion, trying to focus his eyes.

His suit turned completely on, lights came on. He looked around at his data screens, scrolled through menus, thanks to his bio-mechanical integration, and stopped at 'PROXIMITY SCAN.' His data screen displayed: `Monica 2488: 85.356338% rehab.`

"Monica?" he inquired. After a moment he called out, "Calvin?" He scrolled back to 'DAMAGE INVENTORY' on his data screen. The resulting diagnostic that displayed his suit layout labeled it intact and operable, at least mechanically speaking. There was one item blinking in red that indicated the ENET-1 error in his telecommunications systems. This was a hardware issue, but not mechanical. He scrunched his eyes shut and grunted.

Not much had changed in the landscape of sand dunes and buried soldiers until a pile of sand moved. An 'L' shape rose from underneath, displacing sand from its surface; it revealed itself as an arm, then a hand. The hand crawled over the sand, surveying the situation, and then braced itself. As the arm straightened out more sand poured off of Angus. He adjusted his position and exhumed himself from the sand by pushing up with both arms. Sand cleared away and his faceplate was no longer opaque and rusty. A cooling system activated and immediately defogged his faceplate. The bright daytime landscape flooded his vision. He climbed out from the sand, sat up and slowly looked around.

Tracks. Angus could see footprints that led away from the battlefield, left by those repaired soldiers that had completed their rehabilitation.

Another pile was nearby. He crawled over to it and brushed away sand, revealing Monica 2488's battered helmet. The faceplate was intact. Her eyes were closed. He scanned her: `Monica 2488: 85.356338% rehab`. For some reason, her rehabilitation was not proceeding.

Crouching close to her, Angus looked at her unconscious face. Her eyes moved under her eyelids. He cocked his head, as if he found that somehow strange. He tugged on her. She barely moved. He scooted closer, got better leverage and rolled her over. Small lights went on in her helmet. Sand poured off revealing her suit to be intact; apparently, she hadn't suffered any obvious damage in the blast. Angus sat back and thought.

"Buddha? Angus reporting ninety-nine point nine,

nine, nine, seven, three percent rehab. Ready," Angus attempted again, in spite of his previous frustrating experiences. But there was no response. He thought some more. He referred to his data screens:

```
BUDDHA Telemetry Network
Inquiry: Why no response?
```

He waited, then his screen displayed:

```
DAMAGE INVENTORY!
Telemetry broken. Malfunction in ENET-1
microprocessor.
Inquiry: Nature of ENET-1 malfunction?
**No transmission of recognition codes.
[RECOGNITION CODES: Transmitted codes
that allow BUDDHA (Binomial-UUDynamic
Datamated Heuristic Algorithm) to
recognize parties in communication.
Required for data recognition.]
```

He tried again, "Buddha. Angus reporting ninety-nine point nine, nine, nine, seven, three percent rehab. Ready." Nothing. The answer to his query meant little to him. He understood it on a purely informational basis, but on an empirical level he had difficulty accepting that he had a major breakdown in communication. Whether Buddha was interested or not, Angus wasn't getting through.

Angus looked at Monica 2488, stood up and walked

around her. He studied the tracks around them. Apparently many soldiers were back online and left judging by the telltale footprints and single-minded tracks. These stood out in stark contrast to Monica 2488's prone and disabled form in the sand. He watched her faceplate fog with her breath as she lay there.

Angus continued to walk around her in his searching spiral pattern. His sweeps took him progressively away from Monica 2488 to the ridge where he looked back toward the Tower, or where the Tower had been. Long, black smears radiating from ground zero lay where soldiers had been. Nearby, on the wrong side of the ridge, were metal blobs, scorched and melted soldiers that still retained enough physical integrity to betray their previous forms. Their remains lay buried, melted or pooled.

Angus stared at the nearest melted dead. Their bodies were blackened inside their suits, carbonized in an instant. The suits had bubbled from the heat and were distorted by the shockwave of the explosion. It was as if these soldiers had been made of wax and were pulled out of shape in an instant of agony. One soldier's arm remained upright, reaching for safety. What used to be intricate, defined and articulated armor now looked like an expressive but free-form artistic bronze casting with one side covered in smooth glass. Closer to the blast epicenter the sand had been turned into a blackened star of glass in the shape of a huge bowl.

Angus stared at this surreal landscape of figures. His expression was odd. It was as if he was aware that this was meaningful, but he didn't know why. He continued on his radial walk that now took him back over the ridge and away from the blast center.

A proximity alert audio signal went off startling Angus. He turned around quickly, searching for the source. His suit displayed trajectories and a reticle, projected on his faceplate, showing him where to look. But he was caught off-guard and it took him a moment to pay attention.

Finally he focused and saw a dot in the distance, on the horizon. His data screen displayed:

```
PROXIMITY ALERT! PROXIMITY ALERT

    Approaching Colonial Militant
  Transmitting Peace code ^82/*60
        FRIENDLY CONFIRMED!
```

Angus perked up and squinted at the far-off figure that his data screen identified as 'ELDON 0821.' "... Eldon..." Angus muttered to himself. Eldon 0821 was a pinprick in the distance. Even the zoomed-in enlargements of the approaching soldier displayed on some of his data screens were just wavy, mirage-like images of what could be a human being walking toward him. In fact, these images slenderized the human form, removing the clunky, augmented quality definitive of a Colonial Militant.

Angus stepped forward, reflexively. "Greetings, Eldon," he said to the far-off figure. There was no response. Instead, Angus watched Eldon 0821 approach gradually, slowly, step-by-step. Angus continued his walk until he stopped at a point in his arc that would probably coincide with the straight trajectory of the approaching soldier.

"Greetings, Eldon," Angus repeated. Nothing. Angus watched the soldier continue to approach. He was walking directly toward Angus, gradually appearing bigger. Dust and heat waves obscured him. Closer. Bigger. Clearer. It took some time.

Angus was transfixed by what he saw. The far-off figure was becoming a distinct person, a soldier at least, right in front of his eyes. He was transforming with each plodding step from a nebulous mass of color and reflection to a distinctly armored soldier. Even from this distance it was clear that Eldon 0821's armor was shiny, pristine. Angus stared at him patiently with a growing anticipation. Angus would blink and continue to stare at the approaching soldier who had now become clear enough to see. Angus saw Eldon 0821's head inside his huge helmet. He was staring directly ahead of himself, completely unconcerned with Angus or his calls to him.

Eldon 0821's trajectory brought him close enough for

Angus to easily read his markings: Eldon 0821. He wore salvaged armor but it was clean and polished; he was new, right off the assembly line, unlike the dull, orange peel armor of Angus and his colleagues. Big PetroCom logos had been painted on Eldon 0821's legs, arms, shoulders and helmet.

Angus blinked. "Greetings —" Angus faltered. Eldon 0821 was under ten meters away. Eldon 0821 was barely a young man, a teenager still. Whether he knew it or not, Angus was looking at himself when he was twenty years younger. Except for his youth, he was an exact replica of Angus. But he could not remember having ever seen the baby face or the shiny new armor.

Likewise, Eldon 0821's data screens showed a layout of Angus. As far as he was concerned, Angus was definitely there, obliquely in front of him, with a whole list of physical attributes. But there was no name. No received codes. No Peace codes. No Hostile codes. And so Angus didn't exist to Eldon 0821. Or, to be more precise, Angus was as evident as the rock that was buried under the sand with its top 12.76 percent poking through the surface, or as apparent as any of the other objects in the surrounding area that he should be aware of, lest he trip over them.

And so Eldon 0821 seemed to be about to walk past Angus. Angus abruptly stepped in front of him. Eldon 0821 stopped. He blinked a few times, staring at Angus' face without really seeing him. Eldon 0821's data screens displayed Angus' information. They showed him a layout of Angus standing right in front of him, but there was no name. Eldon 0821 took another step, to the side, to continue on his way.

"Greetings," Angus tried again. Still nothing. Eldon 0821 took another step.

Angus reached out and touched Eldon 0821 on the arm. Eldon 0821 looked at Angus and asked, "Who are you?" Angus was taken aback by the sudden acknowledgment.

"Tycho Muhammad,..." Angus stared at Eldon 0821's face. It was smooth and rosy whereas Angus' was creased, drawn and weathered. It was like looking into a strange mirror, something Angus had never done before, or couldn't remember doing. "Angus. 7873," he said to Eldon 0821 and touched him again. It seemed to be the only way to get Eldon 0821 to respond to him.

"You are not...identified," Eldon 0821 said to him.

"Negative. No, that's not true. Angus sev,..." he paused. "Angus," he said, finally, insistently. Eldon 0821 looked around and saw in the distance the various soldiers rehabilitating, including Monica 2488. Angus touched him again. Eldon 0821 thought. "You are not identified," he said again and turned to continue on his way.

"Angus. Angus," Angus said insistently. Eldon 0821 walked away following the same direction as before.

"Wait. Stop. Eldon," Angus said. Eldon 0821 ignored him. "Where are you going?" Angus asked him.

In a sudden change of demeanor Eldon 0821 turned dramatically and, as if he were in a television commercial, enthusiastically said, "Forward. Secure and hold for PetroCom. Look for the blue sky." He then turned back and continued walking.

Angus was exasperated. "Wait. Don't go," he paused, waiting for a response. Eldon 0821 ignored him. "Don't go. Don't leave," Angus pleaded. Eldon 0821 trudged away. "Eldon. Eldon," Angus called after him with lesser and lesser frequency. "Eldon?" And just as gradually Eldon 0821 became a dot on the opposite end of the horizon. Angus watched until the dot wavered out of existence.

Angus looked down at the ground, thinking. Conclusive thoughts occurred to him as he would shift and start to turn, only to stop and reconsider. Then a clear recollection caught his full attention. He looked back at the ridge where Monica 2488 lay amidst his earlier spiraling tracks. Angus set out, walking a straight line back to her.

Monica 2488's data screen indicated her diagnostic procedure was still stalled. Angus looked down at her. She was holding at '85.356338% rehab.'

"Monica," he said, plaintively. Another of his screens displayed:

◇◇◇

```
       Inquiry: Monica 2488 rehab at
               85.356338%.
       Estimated time to 100% rehab.
       REPAIR MODE ERROR (28.2633433)
       [ERROR 28.2633433: Repair routine
       cannot proceed as directed. Start
   again or refer to external diagnostics
           (BUDDHA.rm286.332).]
```

◇◇◇

She had 'crashed' and needed a hard reboot. "Monica? Monica?" he kept calling her name as he knelt next to her and looked at her face. Her eyes were still moving under her eyelids. He scrolled down to his own repair mode and selected it. His repair crabs emerged and sniffed around for chores. But finding nothing they simply returned to the sconces and went dormant.

Angus tried that again and plucking one of the repair crabs he placed it on Monica 2488 trying to direct its attention to her. It twittered around on her shoulder and then simply crawled away from her and back up Angus to its sconce.

Angus watched her for a while. He didn't know how he could fix her. He looked up. Eldon 0821 was gone. He had disappeared, but his tracks trailed behind him.

Angus looked back down at Monica 2488. An expression crossed her face. Weird, he seemed to think. He crouched closer to look. He watched. Another expression. Few and far between more expressions appeared on her face. He was astonished. Angus made an inquiry on his data screen:

◇◇◇

```
        Inquiry: Face Movements?
 Involuntary muscle contractions due
to peripheral cerebral activity during
    ROD (read only dream) states . No
 significance. All critical and/or Hi-
Cap brain activity directed by BUDDHA
  or built-in BUDDHA sub-directories.
```

◇◇◇

Another expression. The corners of Monica 2488's mouth rose; a faint smile. Angus stared at her, watching someone dream, for real, for the first time in his life.

He reached out and touched her helmet. There was nothing that he could think of to do. He didn't know the full extent of her state of disrepair and he didn't know where to start looking, beyond what he had already learned and done.

Movement caught his eye and he glanced up. Far away, in the canyon mouth, another soldier stood up and communicated his rehabilitation. Angus stared at the small figure as it received its confirmation and proceeded to walk away. Angus perked up; perhaps this soldier could help. But as he opened his mouth to say something, he stopped.

The soldier walked in a straight line across the tracks left by Eldon 0821, heading out into the desert. Eldon 0821's appearance and his tracks fascinated Angus. He studied the tracks, followed them, horizon to horizon. Angus stood and stared at the first tracks.

He hesitated, unsure. He looked all around. At the sky. The sun. The twin neighboring moons. The ground. And back to the tracks. Eldon 0821's newest tracks were not as interesting to Angus as those that had brought him here. Perhaps Angus understood that he knew as much about these tracks and what lay ahead of him as Eldon 0821 — nothing — whereas Eldon 0821 had definitely come from somewhere. There was a basic certainty there and perhaps that was more valuable.

And so Angus looked down at Monica 2488 and made a decision. He turned and followed the first tracks to look for Eldon 0821's origin.

TRACKING

The flat terrain was skirted in the distance by mountain ridges and geologic structures. As the hours passed, Angus was exposed to the indifferent beauty of his planet. It didn't occur to him that way, but part of his mind did take notice of the land. His legs were long compared to his own human legs, and even at a casual gait he covered a substantial amount of ground with relative ease. The landscape changed gradually, but it consistently provided new vistas. Much like the sunrise he witnessed, these new images had a novel quality about them.

Even the tracks Angus was following changed. Angus stared at Eldon 0821's footprints as they curved around a huge wreckage half-buried in the sand ahead. This was definitely noteworthy.

Angus gave up on following the footprints for a while and approached the wreckage. Eldon 0821 had completely avoided it and continued on his original course. Angus couldn't do that.

This was another huge ship, but a human transport this time. This was recognizable *human* technology, not alien, as in that other ship Angus had quickly investigated. A name was painted on the side: GeoConSo — Geo-Consolidated. The ship had broken into two pieces. Nose here, storage and propulsion were about two hundred meters away. Laser scars crisscrossed it, especially the engines. Apparently it had been shot down.

Angus stared at it and the obvious damage. The nose section was badly damaged, having taken the brunt of the impact. The ancient remains of a gash in the planet surface, formed by the crashing ship, trailed out behind it, smoothed over by years of blasting winds. After some deliberation and scanning, Angus moved to the hull.

He entered the nose section first, not through a portal, but through a gaping tear on the hull. The floor of the nose section was buckled from the damage of the crash. He struggled forward and scrambled through the corridors until he found the bridge. The ship's design allowed room for soldiers like him to move throughout with some freedom.

In the center of the crumpled nose section he found

a bridge nest, a pod containing the ship's control stations. Four pilots were strapped into their flight seats in the nest. The pilots, wearing spacesuits with GeoConSo patches on them, had been mangled in the crash. The human bodies looked tiny compared to Angus in his permanent oversized armored home.

Angus leaned in and peered into a faceplate. A skull grinned back at him. It was black and shiny, almost polished, and it was very old.

One pilot's head had been crushed in the crash by equipment that collapsed on him or her. Dust and sand were now everywhere. Indirect light from outside, permeating through a tear in the fuselage, filled the area.

Angus made his way out of the ship and walked over to the aft section. The fuselage was listing at a slight angle. The engines had broken off from the fuselage and were bent upward. One of Angus' data screens indicated higher radiation in the aft section as he got closer. He could see a cut-away view of the ship, hull, storage, pressure tanks, wiring, insulation, etc. There were three levels to the transport. Angus climbed into the wreckage and went through a corridor until he found all of the storage bays. They were empty. He found a ladder to the other levels and went upstairs.

In the upper level Angus found a large room. In the corner was a body in a pressure suit. He looked into the faceplate; another grinning, blackened, desiccated skull. Angus turned to the rest of the room.

Sand covered everything.

He moved over to a computer terminal and brushed aside some sand and dust. Lights were still on! The core power system was still functional. The crash had only destroyed the propulsion system, not the ship's automatic power source. He brushed more dust off of the large computer display. Someone had put a sticker on the console that said, HAVE A NICE SOLAR CYCLE! There was too much dust for Angus to wipe away effectively with his huge paw and his detail hand was too small for the task. Angus looked around for something else to use.

He approached the dead crewman, turned him over easily and took a canister off his back. The crew, at the first sign of an attack, had probably donned their helmets in case their ship sprung a leak. He disconnected the canister from the crewman's suit and went back to the console.

With one hand Angus opened the valve and sprayed pressurized air left in the canister over the console and blew the dust away. It effectively revealed more stickers, placed by philosophical crew members: ARE YOU WORKING TO LIVE, OR LIVING TO WORK?, THIS IS THE FIRST SOLAR CYCLE OF THE REST OF YOUR LIFE and PROCESS LOVE, NOT WAR.

He sat down at the terminal. The screen was pale, faded. It displayed a blinking red 'COLLISION ALERT.' Part of the console was shiny, as reflective as a mirror.

As Angus moved he caught his own reflection but ignored it.

He paused and leaned back into the posture that had caused his reflection. He blinked at himself, perplexed. Whether this was the first time he had seen his own reflection or whether it was the first time he had noticed seeing it was unclear. But he was taking notice now.

He leaned in closer, getting a better look. He stared at his eyes for a long moment and then studied his face: the wrinkles, the contours, the flaking sunburnt skin. He leaned back and watched the reflection alter with his movements. He recalled Eldon 0821 and saw his image in his mind. Again, whether he connected the two dots was unclear. But he noticed some important connection between the two of them.

Inadvertently, he bared his teeth and then opened his mouth. He was doing what every human being has done when presented with their reflection, and some privacy. He was testing it, seeing if it indeed belonged to him. He was studying it and how it looked when he did this or that. Smiles were not in his repertoire. Instead, grimaces and scowls came most naturally to him, in addition to simply opening and closing his mouth. As he became more involved in his reflection and his movements he turned his head to see another, more objective, angle of himself. That's when he saw the blinking red 'COLLISION ALERT' screen again.

That brought him back to his initial agenda and he sheepishly turned away from the shiny surface.

Angus touched a key on the console. The alert disappeared. But the red alert had been burnt into the screen after so much time. It could still be seen over the main menu that had replaced it.

Angus grabbed a metal nipple on his armor. He pulled it out and a cable followed. He plugged the cable into a standard jack on the console. The main menu from the ship's console was now also on Angus' data screens; he had tapped into the ship's computer banks.

"Hi, Angus 7873. May I help you?" a voice spoke to him. Angus was stunned by the voice talking to him, recognizing him. It was the ship's computer speaking to him, a business-like, but pleasant female voice. He moved his lips, not knowing what to say.

"You have successfully patched into my data port. Unless otherwise indicated, I will upload primary inventory directories in ten seconds," she said. The screen on the console and Angus' data screens displayed the question: Upload inventory directories? Okay/ Cancel.

Angus didn't know what to do as the screens counted down. The screens flashed as they began to transfer data to him. He flinched as his mind and augmented systems began filling with the new data. The screens were reflected on his faceplate as he absorbed more and more data. His eyes opened wider and wider. His big armored hands twitched as screens flashed by faster and faster. His head started to pull back, his eyes opening wider. He turned his head reflexively away from the console.

◇◇

"it's all here,"...sometimes people have to wait for hours,... the campaign took three months to complete — a failure by any standard,..."What can you buy for a dollar these days?,"...motivates the pistons that then rotate the drive shaft,...some equipment charges may apply,...landing in the outer islands before ever seeing the mainland,...the four basic food groups,..."Watson! I want you,"... regional transmissions of funds,... high temperatures made that impossible,..."The console, the console!"...they hadn't anticipated an attack from the East,...with all of the servers overloaded,... cloning genetic material incapable of reproduction,...and northern hemisphere conditions that could fluctuate as much as eighty degrees,...cerulean blue to adamantine red,..."five thousand, three hundred ships,"...genomic models spliced with synthetic code,...a knuckle-ball pitch,... worsted wool and cotton blend,... high fructose content,...thirty- three and a third,...sixty rounds

```
   a minute¬...across the English
Channel¬...fountain¬ gable roof¬...
  plum pudding¬...tab-separated¬...
   emulsion¬...cheap pulp paper¬...
```

His eyes started to roll back into his head. He was absorbing too much data too quickly. His hands and arms twitched repeatedly in pathetic attempts to press some button to cancel the flow. On the data screens alerts flashed.

^^ SYSTEM OVERLOAD ^^

The data streamed in without interruption, sending Angus into a seizure-like condition. Angus passed out.

"Primary inventory directories successfully uploaded. What would you like to know?" the ship's computer asked.

The voice echoed slightly in the dead room. Angus lay slumped in the large chair designed for soldiers like him. The ship waited patiently as Angus remained unconscious.

GEOCONSO
ANNUAL REPORT

After some time Angus opened his eyes, dazed and confused. He blinked and took stock of his surroundings. He seemed hung over or somehow altered. He stayed there for a while studying his surroundings. The data screens showed him an interface indicating all of the directories on the ship's available hard drives. Angus regained a greater state of consciousness after several minutes with an idea in mind.

"Accessing Flight Record. Flight Record. What would you like to know about Flight Record?" the ship's computer said. His thoughts, his questions, were immediately read and answered by the ship's computer, thanks to the patch connecting them. His data screens showed the complete files, directories and video images available as the ship selected the Flight Record and displayed it for Angus.

◇◇

```
>> FLIGHT RECORD <<
0500:30:01.20; Departure from GeoConSo
Plant 59
MISSION; Return Home GcX32w3.
Nominal flight performance.
^To GeoConSo Largo Earth Station 33^
^^To GeoConSol, Earth^^
*
0500:35:14.48; Engage enemy aircraft.
No escort
*
0500:35:57.77; Mayday transmission
to GeoConSo Plant 59 and GeoConSo
Largo Earth Station. Evasive action
subroutines.
*
0500:37:33.88; Heavy damage, direct
hits on starboard engines.
*
0500:38:43.80; Engine failure. 40% loss
of flight worthiness.
*
0500:39:00.23; Crash. All (10) crew-
members expired. 0 Cargo.
*
>> End flight record. <<
```

◇◇

The record described an unprovoked attack by enemy interceptors on this transport ship. The ship's computer narrated the Flight Record, "Mission: return home.

Departure, solar time, thirty, zero, one, twenty. Nominal flight perfor —" She interrupted her narration as she skipped ahead in response to Angus' thought. "Accessing final log. GeoConSo Transport 5430 crashed at solar time thirty-nine, zero, zero, twenty-three, after being attacked by PetroCom escort ships. All ten crewmembers perished. No rescue/salvage attempt —" she interrupted as she again accessed other files. One data screen showed footage of the attack, the crash and the subsequent hours and days from the ship's cameras. The cameras were placed in positions similar to machine gunners on old World War II bombers. According to the video the transport had been in low orbit, still in the planet's indifferent atmosphere, the sky only slightly darkened by space. It showed the enemy ships closing on the transport and firing accurately on it. The aft camera showed a ship firing from behind and hitting the transport's engines and propulsion section. The subsequent images skipped ahead to sections showing the transport losing altitude while fighting to stay aloft and hoping to get away from its attackers.

Close to the ground another interceptor fired on the ship. The video record was interrupted as Angus scrolled to a line item: MISSION; Return Home GcX32w3. "Mission profile, return home. GeoConSo 5430 was on return flight to GeoConSo Largo Earth Station, GeoConSo1, Earth, according to order GcX32w3 —" she interrupted herself again.

One data screen showed the transport taking off. The ship's computer responded to Angus' thoughts and flashed another screen:

◇◇◇

```
        MISSION DETAIL:
    GcX32w3; Return Home.
Recall all transport and non-planetary
   equipment. GCS Order 8685.335.
```

◇◇◇

"Order GcX32w3, return home, according to GCS Order 8685.335 —" she filled in helpfully. The transport had clearly left the planet for a reason. Angus had now accessed the reason.

"Accessing GCS Order 8685.335. GCS Order 8685.335; All movable personnel and equipment recalled in compliance with CANCELLATION of Terraforming operation on CEM.4 (A.Centauri system 187)," she explained.

Angus thought for a long while. Then she spoke, in response to his silence, "Standing by —" only to interrupt herself by asking, "May I help you — What would you like to know — ," as she caught up to his thoughts.

The data screens displayed more information: CANCELLATION of Terraforming operation. "GCS Comm. 7778743 Last Communication: Terraforming Operation Cancellation. All GeoConSo terraforming operations on CEM.4 have been cancelled. Current transports are redirected — ," she said.

"For further information I recommend the following files," the ship's computer added. Angus contemplated the current screen as she read them to him:

GCS COMM. 7778743:
GcX32w
GCS Order 8685.33
Evac
Plant Shutdown
GCS Annual Report

"Accessing Annual Report," the ship's computer replied to Angus' mental request. Angus' faceplate went opaque as the annual report was projected on it.

Another appealing woman's voice, the Annual Report, read the copy of the annual report with perfect tone and manner. The accompanying video images were beautiful and very colorful. "The GeoConSolidated Annual Report, 2322 Reaching to the stars for a better life on Earth," the Annual Report said. The report was designed for shareholders, not soldiers.

"Contents: Letter to our Shareholders, Annual Report, Statements of Operations, Balance Sheets, Assets, Liabilities and Shareholders' Equity, and Future Plans," the Annual Report said. "Letter to our Shareholders," the Annual Report interrupted, in response to another unspoken selection on Angus' part.

A video began of an enthusiastic and smiling

pudgy white man in a suit and tie, GCS' chief executive officer in his fifties. His name, Wesley Foeghaard, was superimposed on the image. Smiles were new to Angus. His face inadvertently mimicked one. He had never seen a man in his fifties, nor had he seen many smiling, as far as he could recall.

"Dear...Angus 7873:" Mr. Foeghaard said, as the video image made his lips mimic the words he apparently was saying. This was a nice feature that customized annual reports to the shareholders who read them. He paused before continuing, "I am very happy to say that last year proved to be —"

Angus stopped the video and stared at this strange phenomenon. This was the oldest man he had ever seen, dressed in the oddest way. He was used to seeing men and women inside armored atmosphere suits who were aged and weather beaten. This man was practically as pink as a piglet, except that Angus didn't know what a piglet was.

A portion of the video replayed. "I am very happy to say — ," it stopped and rewound. "I am very happy — ," it stopped and rewound. "I am — ," it stopped and rewound. "I — ," and it stopped and rewound again. Angus stared at him and tried saying "...I..." And then he stared into space, thinking.

"I am very happy to say that last year proved to be a great year for GeoConSolidated, witnessing an 89 percent increase in overall operations, up from our 65 percent increase the year before. Net sales for the year ending December 31, 2322,..." Mr. Foeghaard continued. Angus' faceplate and his data screens were coordinated in a startling multimedia symphony, illustrating the information of the annual report.

"Moving on," the Annual Report said. As with the ship's computer, the Annual Report interrupted Mr. Foeghaard and moved on to other items, according to Angus' interest. Mr. Foeghaard resumed further along, "...continue from changes the company instituted ten years ago. Seeking strategic opportunities and new product developments to enhance the company's growth..."

"Moving on," the Annual Report interrupted again.

"...Sometimes, to continue as a healthy endeavor, one must clear away old growth and make room for the new. Some operations deemed unprofitable have been phased out; the Jovian Asteroid Belt Station, the Great Alaskan Oil Fields and several outer world operations. These moves have contributed to the company's profitability,..." Mr. Foeghaard continued. Angus watched video snippets of the Jovian Asteroid Belt Station, the Great Alaskan Oil Fields and the outer world operations.

The "outer world operations" looked a lot like the planet Angus knew, including terraforming plants and towers. Wesley's margarine smile was interrupted by the Annual Report as she listed the contents, "Moving on.

Annual Report. An overview on GeoConSo's operations. Fossil fuels and mining throughout the known universe."

The annual report was introduced by a montage of glitzy pictures of happy people working and playing. Apparently, GeoConSo made lots of people happy, smiles everywhere. A smiling man and a woman (and smaller versions of both of them, children) were on a deck that was part of a big white structure — a house. There were lots of windows and works of art on the walls.

The four people, the family, looked at the planets in the sky, in the blue sky. Angus stared at the blue sky. He was acquainted with a sky the color of rust. The blue looked funny to him, as it had in the dream he shared with the other soldiers.

Now the family was on a beautiful beach. The woman was wearing a bikini. Angus stared at her body. *His hand on the small of her back.* His huge armored hand twitched to his foreign memory. "The work that GeoConSo does makes all of this possible," the Annual Report proclaimed.

The Annual Report ran down a list of accomplishments as shown. "New refinery techniques perfected by GeoConSo," was narrated to images of sunsets and silhouettes of smokestacks. "Lunar operations," labeled images of personnel working in structures on Earth's moon. "The gas giants: energy research," was illustrated by space workers smiling stupidly, orbiting Jupiter and Saturn. "Military research and development," was punctuated visually by gung-ho and technoid photographs. "Deep space operations." This stopped Angus cold. It was a picture of a shiny, brand new soldier like Angus, but not like Angus; it was not soldered and welded together from salvaged pieces, but factory-made, brand new. Newer than Eldon 0821 even.

This other soldier was heroic as he towered on a desolate planet in a binary system; two suns in the background. He actually looked like a younger Calvin 6501. There were more soldiers behind him. In the background, peeking through clouds, was a tower. As Angus looked at it, the Annual Report captioned it, "Terraforming Oxygenation Plants." Angus was transfixed...As familiar as he was with his own world, this moment only showed him how little he knew it.

"Terraforming plants and refineries are placed on dead planets with oxygen rich soils in an effort to return them to Earth-like splendor. In a short time these planets are ready for use in our massive colonization effort," the Annual Report enthused. An animated diagram showed how the Towers took oxygen in the planet's soil, converted it to gas and pumped it into the atmosphere. The animation showed the rebirth of an entire planet, sped up for our edification.

"GCS' Colonial Militia helps secure these planets for exclusive use by GCS brand colonies. Against competing companies like PetroCom, InfraSpace, ExxoCon, and others, the Colonial Militia graciously provides an invaluable service," the Annual Report said. The annual report showed shiny happy Colonial Militants, by the thousands, lining up to board transport ships, much like the one Angus was in.

All of the faces of the Colonial Militants were the same faces he had seen in all of his battles, the same faces as Calvin 6501, Eustus 2190, Strunz 3197, Leni 2221, Monica 2488, and his own. His face twitched involuntarily as he watched the parade, slightly stunned. Recognition and irrecognition wrestled within Angus.

The animation showed a sanitized version of the massive colonization effort. Landing on a desolate planet and claiming it was illustrated by an animated field of color with the GeoConSo logo spreading over the planet and obliterating the competitors' logos. Hundreds of towers now worked, terraforming this hypothetical planet into a beautiful distant cousin of Earth. "Six operations have so far proven to be great successes," the Annual Report cooed.

The image of thousands of Towers spewing vapors was almost identical to 20th century footage of factories polluting the Earth's atmosphere, but these were making lethal atmospheres breathable.

Another picture showed a Tower with a puffy white plume growing out the top, with green grass and trees growing around the plant and refinery, framed by a brilliant blue sky.

The shiny new Colonial Militant stood triumphant, without his helmet, in this new world (something Angus knew he should never do). "Colonial Militants are men and women specially trained for their valued service," the Annual Report continued. Angus recalled the Defender, Roach 9901, with his helmet torn off, breathing the atmosphere of this planet, screaming.

"Colonial Militants are administered in their combat activities through the help of our GCS Systems Hologrammatical ONYX computer arrays. As needed, ONYX systems present to the Colonial Militants divine figures, an identity that brings out the most commitment and dedication, such as Buddha, Muhammad, Vishnu, Jesus, and others.

"With militia suits and the telemetry assistance of a central supervisory computer, they combat competing companies. Only the best computer is good enough for our Colonial Militia; the GCS Systems Hologrammatical ONYX," the Annual Report said. Angus' attention returned to a picture of a particularly large Tower complex, apparently with Buddha inside.

"When strategic alliances are formed, ONYX systems can easily and immediately end bellicose operations and form cooperative ventures, allowing for better combat administration," the Annual Report said. The animation showed a hybrid of the GCS logo and a competitor's logo covering the world in friendly coexistence.

A picture of a dish antenna appeared followed by computer animation of a satellite in low orbit. "...Our best orbital satellite model, the OS17, is used to keep all Colonial Militia in constant contact with combat administration," the Annual Report explained.

"Buddha" sent the phrase "This blue sky brought to you by GCS," on a friendly animated lighting bolt to the satellite which then sent it to the waiting shiny new Colonial Militant, which seemed to start up and move into action. The soldier then smiled, waved his huge armored hand and said, "This blue sky brought to you by GCS."

"...look for the blue sky,..." Angus muttered to himself. His jaw clenched. He turned and stared at the ARE YOU WORKING TO LIVE, OR LIVING TO WORK sticker and minutes, perhaps hours, went by.

The Annual Report droned on while Angus gaped. "Some operations have been cancelled due to poor profit projections. Planetary research shows that CAL.6 (A.Centauri system 218) would require a larger effort than GCS is prepared for at this time. CEM.4 (A.Centauri system 187), a long and particularly difficult operation, has been cancelled due to heavy initial investment costs," the Annual Report said, making Angus blink and perk up.

The Annual Report repeated herself in response to

Angus' unspoken, "What?" "CEM.4 (A.Centauri system 187), a long and particularly difficult operation, has been cancelled due to heavy initial investment costs."

He gulped. Another window and menu called up the mission profile. His faceplate cleared up as the Annual Report now displayed on one of the console's screens and his data screens showed him other information. "Mission profile" the ship's computer interjected and then said, "Moving on. GCS Order 8685.335;...CANCELLATION of Terraforming operation on CEM.4 (A.Centauri system 187)."

Angus peered at his screens and the larger console screens in the ship. He read and re-read the information. He leaned closer. The "CEM.4 (A.Centauri system 187)" on the mission profile window and the "CEM.4 (A.Centauri system 187)" on the annual report screen were an exact match. It took Angus a long time to seemingly come to a conclusion; this was the same planet Angus had lived and fought on his whole life.

Angus opened a third window and went back to the GCS Comm. 7778743 Last Communication menu:

```
         GCS COMM. 7778743*
              *GcX32w*
        *GCS Order 8685.33*
               *Evac*
          *Plant Shutdown*
        *GCS Annual Report*
```

He accessed "*Evac*."

"EVACuation order: Terraforming operation planet CEM.4 (in the Alpha Centauri, system 187) is to be evacuated of all transport and non-planetary equipment and personnel. All Colonial Militia and terraforming plants are losses and to be left behind," the ship's computer said in a perfunctory way.

Angus blinked a few times.

Angus thought a new question. The computer's words chipped away at Angus' expression, "Cancel: 1) verb: to give up something previously arranged or agreed on. Call off, drop, scrub, end, terminate, annul, invalidate, rescind, revoke, give up, relinquish, surrender. 2) verb: to eliminate or neutralize with or as if with a stroke of the pen. Erase, annul, black out, blot out, delete, efface, expunge, obliterate, wipe out, X-out, negate, nullify, abolish, blank out, cross off, cross out, cut out, eliminate, excise, extirpate, rub out, scrape, sponge out, strike out, neutralize, remove, take out, withdraw — ."

Another question occurred to him impelling the ship's computer to access another definition. The words eroded what little confidence and self-esteem Angus had. "Left behind: 1) phrase: something or someone that had not been gathered, collected, picked up, included, remembered, valued, appreciated. As in garbage, refuse, debris, trash, unwanted materials, discard. 2) Phrase: forgotten, overlooked, neglected, missed —" the ship's computer interrupted its list.

Angus looked back at the annual report. "...operation had been cancelled due to heavy initial investment costs," she said.

Angus digested what he just learned. His expression fluttered between unfamiliar thoughts and pains. He was like a faulty TV with the vertical hold scrolling repeatedly for a long time.

"Would you like anything else, Angus 7873?" the ship's computer finally asked. Angus snapped out of his fugue and seemed to glare at the ship's computer.

REPAIRS

It was nighttime. The neighboring twin planets were waxing, at a quarter now, as Angus diligently walked away from the crash site. The planets cast a strange violet light on everything. Angus' helmet lights were on, shining the two white ovals in front of him as he followed his tracks back the way he had come.

The wind was fairly strong. Sand pelted him from the side. It hissed as he leaned into it. Fortunately, Angus had his tracks superimposed on his faceplate, showing him the way back. Still, his old, heavy footprints did remain in the ground, despite the wind.

Angus had an odd expression on his face, one of deep concentration, almost anger, as he stared in front of himself. He wasn't concentrating on anything in particular. For a while on the long walk, Angus stared at the time counter again: seconds, minutes, hours, days, weeks, months, years; seconds, minutes, hours, days, weeks, months, years...He didn't really need to look where he was going, particularly for most of the flat terrain ahead of him. But had he looked around, he would have seen the eerie beauty of his world at night. The bright planets shined enough by night to cast deep shadows around him from rocks, undulations in the terrain and himself, of course. The result was a purplish, dappled terrain that dissipated into the nighttime of space.

Angus was a tiny set of lights in the vast violet expanse as he followed his tracks across the flat terrain. The twin planets seemed to look down on him as forlorn minders. Tiny Angus simply walked and walked to his next objective, all alone.

Angus' eyes pulled away from his screens and he finally looked out at the world around him. The look of tension or anger had subsided slightly in his face. But thoughts were clearly coursing through his mind as he traveled. He looked at the planets hanging in the sky and spotted some stars near them. It took Angus a while before he thought a new idea. His head lamps went off and his eyes acclimated to the darkness. He was in no danger of losing his way. He looked out of his darkened helmet and saw the sky more clearly. The stars were easier to see now and there were many, many more of them.

Angus' jaw dropped a bit as he stared at the sight. His gait slowed down in response to his astonishment until he came to a complete stop. He stared out at the night sky and slowly turned around, creaking and whirring as his suit moved. There was an eerie serenity around him. It was the silence of desertion. There was nothing and no interest in anything here. There were no minds or thoughts that gave any consideration to these hills and this terrain or the twin planets that arced across the sky. Except for Angus' mind.

He stared at the landscape until he returned to his tracks and remembered his objective. He spotted some fairly distinct tracks still in the sand, his tracks. He bent over to look at them more clearly. They were walking toward him, of course, and they met him at the point where he stood. He had a suspicion that there was something meaningful in this quaint tableau, of standing face to face with his own footsteps.

Angus straightened and continued walking. His massive feet smeared his earlier tracks as he walked forward. He still gazed at the undulating and changing terrain as he slowly made it to the ridge many hours later and found Monica 2488 more buried in the sand than when he had left her.

He knelt down beside her and scanned her: `Monica 2488: 85.356338% rehab`. His data screen indicated life: `Life signs: Stable`. He grabbed one of her arms and dragged her out of the sand. He moved in close and looked at her through the faceplate. The violet light made her scary looking until his helmet lights washed away the violet. Her eyes were still moving under her eyelids. She had drooled a bit.

Standing and reaching back, he pulled out a cable from the back of his suit. He bent down and attached it to a metal loop on Monica 2488's suit. He reached around the other side and did the same thing. He had attached her to his winch system.

He took a step back and squatted down. He hit a switch and the cables winched her closer and dragged her up and onto his back, sand and armor against armor, scraping and screeching. He scooted under her weight, lifting her on his back, and stood up.

He tested his balance; he was a huge Colonial Militant with an equally huge soldier as a burden. He resumed tracing his tracks back the way he had come, this time with a slower gait. His steps were steadier and more careful because of his burden. But in a short amount of time he achieved a smooth robotic rhythm that he kept up for hours.

Angus' footsteps were heavier as he arrived at the crash site much, much later. Despite his augmentation, he was exhausted; carrying a heavy burden still required an extra effort, augmentation or no augmentation. The weather had worsened and worked against him. He strained his way closer to the transport ship. Step by step. Meter by meter. The planets had sunken closer to the horizon.

Finally he reached the crashed transport. He walked around the wreckage and found a series of large service doors on one side marked "Payload." He lowered Monica 2488 next to a payload door closest to the ground. His winches paid out line as he set her down and then he disengaged from her and walked away.

Inside the transport ship a portal slid open and Angus stepped inside. He turned and closed the door. He was in a big, empty bay. Across the bay was the series of payload doors. Angus walked across to a panel on the side of the door where he left Monica 2488 and opened it, letting in the howling wind. Monica 2488 was lying on the sand outside, where he left her. He dragged her inside and closed the door. Then he reconnected the winch cables and dragged her to another door.

This door opened and Angus dragged her inside a smaller room to an angled table that was the shape of a soldier. They were now in a repair room just off of the huge payload bay in the crashed transport ship. Angus then connected himself to the console as he had on the bridge.

"Hi, Angus 7873. May I help you?" the ship's computer recognized him. This startled him again, but he recovered quickly. Angus stood with his back to the head of the angled table and his winch cables attached to Monica 2488 stretching over it. He let his winch hoist her onto the table and then disengaged. He connected her computer link to the table and connected cables from the table to her.

"Hi, Monica 2488. May I help you?" the ship asked. Angus accessed "environmental control" from one of the many data screens available.

"Pressurizing repair room, stand by," the ship said. The room pressurized. Angus then opened a vent in his helmet. Tested the air. He sneezed repeatedly, but it was okay.

"Bless you!" the ship said.

Angus had never sneezed before, not that he could remember. He looked at Monica 2488's face and then sat down at the terminal. "Starting repair mode diagnosis," the ship said. The console screen displayed information:

◇◇

```
Inquiry: Monica 2488 rehab at
         85.356338%
 REPAIR MODE ERROR (28.2633433)
 [ERROR 28.2633433: Repair routine
 cannot proceed as directed. Start
again or refer to external diagnostics
    (BUDDHA.rm286.332).]
```

◇◇

"Monica 2488 is 85 percent functional. Automated repair mode cannot proceed due to an error, error 28.2633433. Organic component requires recuperation as well. What would you like me to —" the ship interrupted herself. "Locating malfunction," she continued.

"CMX 2B microprocessor is burnt out. Would you like to replace —" she interrupted herself again as Angus blinked a thought at her. "Replacing," she confirmed.

The table came to life as repair crabs came out of it and Monica 2488's suit. Repair crabs also came out of the repair room walls. They all scurried over and met at the huge, prone soldier and immediately got to work, evaluating, diagnosing and repairing. A closer look at the repair room walls would have revealed textures similar to those on the armor of the Colonial Militants, both containing the many tiny spaces that held the repair crabs.

As two of the repair crabs opened a hatch on Monica 2488's back, a tiny board popped out. One crab plucked a chip from the circuit board. The other replaced it with a new one it had retrieved from the spare parts cache in the repair room. The board slid back in.

"CMX 2B replaced and operative," the ship said.

Angus looked at Monica 2488 on the table. "Start repair mode, automatic or manual?" the ship asked. Then she confirmed the selection, "Manual."

The computer ran down all of the components and listed them allowing Angus to decide what got repaired. Repair crabs scurried all over Monica 2488. Angus approved everything until it got to the ENET-1 MICROPROCESSOR.

"Reset?" the ship asked just as it had with every single other component. But this time Angus shook his head, no.

"Disabling ENET-1 microprocessor will prevent telemetry control by Buddha of Monica two four, —" the ship interrupted her friendly reminder and then stated, "ENET-1 microprocessor is disabled."

The rest of the repair routine continued for several hours as Angus approved each repair.

*   *   *

A boy, 9, stood wearing a grey jumpsuit with tubes and wires attached to it. He wore a cap with even more wires attached. Laser scan-lines flashed across his face. He watched.

He watched as other children walked along a metal corridor. There were lights, sounds. The whole place was a scary machine.

Then the boy was older, 13, an adolescent like the others around him. He still wore a grey jumpsuit as before. He walked along the metal corridor in a line with other adolescents.

He was in a wire frame version of the Colonial Militia suits, training. A row of adolescents trained at various skills: basic movements, running, and target practice. Their tiny bodies looked like budgies trapped in Edwardian bird cages that had been articulated to fulfill some sick fantasy.

The young man was sleeping. All of them were in capsules, similar to coffins, with caps on their heads, linking them to a central computer. Their eyes moved beneath their lids in hypno-learning.

The young man was in target practice with an apparatus on his arm and head; laser sighting. Laser targets. Other young adults were doing the same thing in vast rows in a huge hangar.

The young man stepped up to a platform, as did all the other adolescents in one rank. A machine effortlessly picked him up and quickly "built" a suit of armor around him. First a metal exoskeleton; hydraulics, pulleys, tendons and joints were assembled around the young man. Then snug-fitting microprocessor boxes and peripheral equipment were attached, followed by articulated armor panels.

Finally three cables were fastened to the back of his head. Sparks. Pain. Then the helmet.

A huge receiving area opened its doors slowly. Outside was an arid plain. From the depths of the room where sliding doors had opened came all of the adolescents in their shiny new armored suits: new Colonial Militants. Young Angus looked up at the sky for the very first time as he stepped outside with the first rank of new soldiers.

He was astonished by the sight as the huge sky loomed over him; something he had never seen before in his limited and isolated life. His youthful face was open to the wonder of this new world as he gazed out. But then computer buffers dampened his curiosity. His face literally shut down from the astonished expression which initially graced his face as he first turned his attention to the plain in front of him.

He wore an utterly blank expression as he paused and raised his right foot, setting out to wander.

Young Angus was an Attacker, fighting Defenders. Laser fire coursed by him, grenades exploded, rockets shot across a battlefield.

As the Attackers pressed their advantage, the Defenders, with help from the Flying Vehicle, neutralized the Attackers.

Some were instantly destroyed. Smoke was everywhere, smoke that drifted away as the battle subsided, smoke that cleared to reveal a Tower.

This Tower was huge. This was where Buddha lived...

And out of the top. NOTHING. Nothing came out of it. No converted oxygen pumped into the atmosphere. No white vapor. No blue sky.

After the battle the field was littered with the injured,

the dying and the dead. Young Angus watched all of them, their faces contorted in pain, crying out. Angus watched and understood very little.

CALIBRATIONS

Angus was asleep with his helmet off. He woke up startled. The same three cables were connected to the back of his head now as when he was younger. His head barely cleared the collar of his armor as he sat against a wall in the repair room.

He stood and saw Monica 2488. Her helmet was also off. She too was bald, their hair follicles had been genetically stunted so they grew at most a feeble fuzz where they should have had hair. She was in rest mode now; the repair table had converted into a chair. Angus shook the sleep out of his head and thought for a while.

He noticed something about her, even though the lights were at half power, scrambled to his feet and got closer. Her face twitched. Monica 2488 was dreaming, but Angus didn't quite know that. Tears had streamed down her face and glistened in the indirect light of the repair room. The reflection made them stand out in stark contrast to everything else. He was fascinated and watched as a new tear emerged from the corner of her eye and then slipped down her cheek.

Angus slowly reached out his armored hand toward her face. His augmented hand could have easily crushed her head. Instead he extended a finger and gently touched the tear. His fingertips had touch sensitive panels. He could "feel" it through his armor and he reacted slightly. *His hand on the small of her back.* The situation suddenly made him self-conscious and he snapped out of it. He stepped back and lowered his hand just in time as she woke.

Incongruously he launched into a good mimicry of the ship computer's enthusiasm, "Hi, Monica 2488.

"Where are we going?" he asked. She gaped at him, recognizing her designation, her name. But she didn't recognize him.

"Forward. Secure and hold for PetroCom," she didn't think, she just said it. In turn, Angus was surprised and stared at her.

"Look for the blue sky..." Angus whispered to himself.

"Buddha. Monica reporting one hundred percent rehab. Ready," Monica 2488 said. She had turned her attention away from Angus and focused instead on completing her rehabilitation routine, announcing her readiness for duty.

There was no response. She periodically looked at Angus, but only because he was standing there, staring at her. "Buddha. Monica reporting one hundred percent rehab. Ready. Respond," she repeated.

"Your ENET-1 is disabled," he told her. She heard what he said and seemed to corroborate that with her own data screens as she ran a quick diagnostic. Despite the fact that he didn't exist to her, there was no reason not to check out what he had said.

She made a decision and accessed a menu to enable her ENET-1. Realizing this Angus raised a hand and said, "Don't!" She paused and looked at him.

"It controls transmissions with Buddha," he added. She checked that too. "Buddha will not respond. Look at something first," he told her with a simple finality. After some consideration she looked at him.

"You were damaged in the last battle," he explained to her. She looked at their surroundings and the fact that her helmet was off. "A GeoConSo transport ship," he volunteered, guessing what her questions were. She gave the place another look.

"...There are no transport ships," she retorted, apparently knowing this much.

"This one is...old...crashed," he explained to her.

Monica 2488 nodded, almost imperceptibly. Angus walked over to Monica 2488. "Look," he said.

"May I help you — accessing," the ship said.

Angus then showed her everything he had learned from the ship's hard drives, with help from the ship computer as it accessed all of the pertinent files. Monica 2488 watched intently: the Colonial Militant from the GeoConSo annual report; the section on terraforming; the flight record; the cancellation order; the OS17 satellite; the list of competitors. He gave her a lot to think about.

"...Against competing companies like PetroCom, InfraSpace, ExxoCon and others, the Colonial Militia graciously provides an..." the ship explained.

Angus interjected, "This is a GeoConSo ship." He stared at Monica 2488. He stepped closer, thinking, and then asked her, "What happened to GeoConSo, InfraSpace and ExxoCon?"

Monica 2488 thought, instead of responding. He looked into her eyes. She looked back at him without any reaction.

"Monica 2488," he said to focus her attention. This way of addressing her threw her off. It was too...personal. Angus was struggling to put together a thought.

"What are you...doing here?" he said. Monica 2488 stared at him.

Angus thought some more and came up with another notion. "What is your mission?" After trying so hard to communicate with Calvin 6501 and Eldon 0821, Angus was determined to get through to Monica 2488.

"Secure and hold for PetroCom," she responded, brightening a little.

He was getting somewhere. "What is that?" he asked, basically. Monica 2488 opened her mouth and then stared at him, but this time she was thinking more.

"Where is PetroCom?" he pursued. Monica 2488 was about to respond but she realized that she didn't know and stopped short. Her facial expression was one of consternation and almost fear as she quickly searched for an answer. Her expression calmed and she became deadpan again as she responded, "That is irrelevant. NCTMP, not-critical-to-mission-performance."

Angus got more worked up. "Then why secure and hold for PetroCom if it is irrelevant?" he debated.

These questions were making her brain hurt. She recalled something and brightened a bit. "To make new worlds and new homes for mankind!" she said a little more triumphantly. Everyone wanted to please, even on the most basic level.

Angus had her now. He had something brilliant to ask her and savored the feeling. He focused on her eyes and asked, "Where are the mankinds?"

Her triumph vanished. Again she was stumped. He turned his attention to the computer files.

"Accessing, GCS Comm. 7778743 last communication,"

the ship said. Angus looked at the console screen:

```
GCS COMM. 7778743:
*GcX32w*
*GCS Order 8685.33*
*Evac*
*Plant Shutdown*
*GCS Annual Report*
```

He scrolled down to *Plant Shutdown.*

"PLANT SHUTDOWN: All terraforming plants shut down according to UN regulation 86356. (No incomplete experiments shall be left unattended.)" the ship narrated.

One of his screens had the list of plants. "Accessing Plant 59: Ready," the ship said.

"Plant 59 operation status, inactive. Accessing. Plant 59 is fully operational," the ship added.

Angus and Monica 2488 stared at the screens. Then the ship went down the whole list, "Accessing. Listing all plants and their operational status: Plant 1: INACTIVE; Plant 2: INACTIVE; Plant 4: INACTIVE; Plant 5: INACTIVE; Plant 6: INACTIVE; Plant 9: INACTIVE; Plant 28: INACTIVE; Plant 29: INACTIVE; Plant 30: INACTIVE; Plant 31: INACTIVE; Plant 32: INACTIVE; Plant 33: INACTIVE; Plant 35: INACTIVE; Plant 36: INACTIVE; Plant 38: INACTIVE —"

Angus was surprised and had stopped the list and spoke to the computer, "Are all plants inactive?"

"Yes," the ship said. Suddenly Monica 2488 looked

at Angus.

"The plants are operational, but they are not operating," he explained to her. She stared back at him. "Terraforming is not happening here," he explained.

"Then, what is...the objective...of...all this?" she asked him. She stared and seemed to search for the words or the explanation or a reason. "Then...why?" she finally asked.

Angus leaned in as close as he could and looked into her eyes. "I...don't...know..."

Monica 2488 had twitched as he said "I."

"We...are fighting...a cancelled operation," he elaborated slowly, picking his words carefully. This time she accessed the cover of the annual report.

"You...are fighting a cancelled operation —" Angus insisted.

"Stop!" she interrupted him. She held up a hand. She was overloaded with information. He stopped and waited, watching her eyes dart around, thinking.

She studied the console screen:

GeoConSolidated
Annual Report
2322

He continued, "There is no blue sky here —"

"What is the current year?" she asked, interrupting Angus. Angus stared back at her. "Don't know —

wait,..." he said. Then he checked his clock on his data screen. Monica 2488 knew for herself as soon as she had thought the question, but she turned to the computer as Angus thought the question.

"Current year is four thousand, two hundred thirty-one, solar time, also known as Earth time. At the tone the time is zero two hundred, twenty-two, thirty-two, and ninety-eight seconds," the ship said. The computer chimed.

"What is the year of the crash of this transport?" Monica 2488 asked.

"Lima year, sixty-seven. Solar year, two thousand, three hundred twenty-two," the ship answered.

"One thousand nine hundred and nine years ago,..." Angus whispered. Monica 2488 and Angus stared at each other.

"How long is that?" she asked.

He looked at her and then shrugged through his armor. "I don't know,..." he said. They looked at each other without really understanding what they had learned....

MONICA

His hand on the small of her back.

Angus woke up. Monica was nearby, asleep. They had their helmets on and were in an upstairs section of the downed transport that had large windows.

A storm outside battered the ship. Angus watched as the atmosphere roiled and thundered. Periodically, lightning cracked down. The wind howled. It rocked the wreckage. It was quite beautiful.

Angus looked at Monica. She was squatting, asleep. He watched her quietly. He looked out the windows again. The clouds were changing. Suddenly a finger of atmosphere started to point down; a funnel cloud.

It formed swiftly, and powerfully. It poked down. As

soon as it touched the ground, it sucked sand into the sky.

The howling, battering wind sandblasted the crashed ship. The funnel reddened more deeply in direct proportion to the amount of sand it sucked. It curved and whipped around seductively.

It started to move toward the ship.

Angus checked his data screens:

◇◇

WARNING!

Cyclonic disturbance!
Move to shelter!

◇◇

Angus stood and moved toward Monica. He touched her. "Monica. Wake up. Monica!" he said.

She woke up with a start, confused, "Huh? Wha... What?"

"A cyclonic disturbance. Stand up," he said. They scrambled away from the windows. The funnel approached the ship quickly and then struck the ship, rocking it violently.

The ship suffered severe damage when it crashed after the attack so many years ago. This section no longer maintained hull integrity, which permitted the buffeting to shake lose bulkheads and seals. After sustained resistance to external pressure, windows bulged inward and exploded.

Various loose objects were sucked out of the ship.

Angus and Monica, despite their weight and size, were pulled off their feet and sucked toward the windows. They scrambled to hold onto anything to save their lives.

Sudden gusts yanked on them even harder, pulling them outside. They both bumped up against the hull, grabbed a hold of the window frames (or what was left of them) and fought against the wind. The funnel slowly pulled them out. They pushed against the hull trying to stay inside, groaning and straining against the immense strength of the cyclone.

Then the hull ripped open.

Angus and Monica shot out of the wreckage and were lifted into the funnel of air, screaming. Their fear was purely instinctive. Data screens were going crazy, flashing warnings at them, basically telling them to get their feet back on the ground. They, however, were tumbling in the air, over and over, as they climbed higher and higher.

"Monica!" Angus yelled.

She even called out his name, "Angus!" The wind lifted them higher in the air and carried them for a moment. The cyclone moved past the ship, having destroyed the portion it touched. Angus and Monica both got glimpses of the strange view from their elevations, making their world seem smaller as well as more expansive. It registered, along with everything else they were experiencing, as strange and remarkable.

These huge Colonial Militants twirled about like toys until they fell to the ground, scattered like the rest of the debris. They crashed in the sand, barely missing fatal damage.

The storm crawled over them, kicking them one or two more times, and gradually died out.

They were breathing heavily, but calmed down in time. Angus had a strained expression on his face. He stared out at what could have been his death. His expression tightened. He was definitely angry.

He tried to push himself up, but fell. His arm was damaged. He grunted and tried the other arm, successfully getting up to look around. He couldn't see Monica anywhere nearby.

She couldn't see Angus either from her new location. They resorted to their data screens. A screen showed them on the map and plotted how far away they were from each other.

Angus stood fully, his damaged arm hung limp. He accessed his repair mode, inciting his repair crabs to emerge and immediately begin repairs on his arm.

"Monica? Are you operational? Were you damaged?" Angus asked.

She referred to her screens. "Negative on damage...I," Monica paused. The word "I" stopped her, but she had said it. "...am operational."

"Excellence. Recommend reconnoiter at azimuth

42.7723." Angus said. Angus reviewed the map that was blinking a spot halfway between them, their recommended meeting point.

"Copy. Are you damaged?" Monica asked.

He checked his diagnosis, "Negative."

Monica heard that and sort of smiled, relieved, "Good..."

They each started walking, following the trajectories plotted on their faceplates, toward each other. Their faceplates indicated the other in the distance as a blinking dot, a blip that lay somewhere behind the landscape in front of them. They had been thrown about a mile away from each other, according to their suits.

Monica could see the cyclone slithering away from her in the sky. At the ground it was still kicking up dust and debris as the funnel wavered along its path. The sight gave her pause.

"What are we going to do?" Monica asked.

Angus looked at her blip on the data screen. From his position he could see the cyclone slinking away as well. His expression seemed to have a new determination to it. There was a set to his jaw as he stared at the retreating galoot that almost killed them. He nodded to himself as he came to a conclusion. "We're going to find Buddha."

Monica's eyebrows arched as her face registered her surprise. She was barely conscious of what that meant to her, but she knew enough to know that "finding Buddha" was exceptional. She thought about it as she walked to their rendezvous and gradually nodded to herself as well. Buddha had always been part of her life. But finding Buddha seemed inappropriate, for some reason, although she couldn't come up with what that reason was. She also couldn't come up with a reason that could possibly keep them from doing so.

Fleeting micro-expressions played on her face as she contemplated everything she had experienced in the last few days. Part of her was definitely happy or eager to see what their future held. And part of her was curiously apprehensive about it. Their instincts, augmented or otherwise, were to make contact with Buddha as soon as they reached one hundred percent rehabilitation. In fact, their instincts to reconnect had nothing to do with the percentage of their operational abilities. It was there as soon as they became conscious of still being operational after battle. So, why wouldn't they try to reconnect in a more direct way, particularly after what Angus had shown her?

A fleeting thought occurred to Monica. She could enable her ENET-1 chip and simply reconnect with Buddha, but something about Angus' plan intrigued her. Perhaps it had something to do with the nature of their relationship. She couldn't recall knowing any other Colonial Militant in quite the same way before. At will, Monica could recall other soldiers, their faces, their designations. In fact, video of them replayed on some of her data screens as she accessed those memories. But those were different. She could not have stated this, but those were simply data, records of past experiences, battles mostly. Angus was different.

Their suits quietly whined and purred as their mechanics moved them along the barren terrain on their way to their meeting. The cyclone was now a reddish smudge in the distance, a dumb rampaging brute on this angry little world.

It took a short while for them to meet. Again, Monica could not have expressed this, nor was she conscious of it, but her vital signs clearly indicated that she had been apprehensive during their separation and only calmed down when she saw Angus walking toward her. He too had a similar reaction, but it was pushed aside by this new feeling of anger he felt ever since their close call.

Nonetheless, as they approached each other and got close enough to see each other with their unaided eyes, they peered at each other with a new level of interest.

They stepped right up to each other, following their trajectories to the last meter, and stopped. An awkward pause occurred then as they looked at each other and seemed to confirm for themselves, despite their many sensors and data screens, that they were, in fact, okay.

Angus called up a trajectory and transferred it to Monica's faceplate. Then he turned and they began walking.

*   *   *

The world had taken a brilliant violet glow as the sun set. Gradually Angus and Monica's helmet lights came on. They continued walking together.

Angus had Eldon 0821's tracks projected onto his faceplate from the replay of when he encountered him. They were following those tracks.

Impressive mountains stood in the distance, evidence of ancient oceans carving this planet and tossing aside enormous ridges of stone and dirt. Both Monica and Angus noticed them in their own quiet manner. Visually impressive experiences were still out of their range of comprehension, but they were starting to notice them.

Angus' repair crabs finished fixing his arm and returned to their homes; some even returned to Monica's armor. Angus tested his repaired arm as the last repair crabs sealed themselves away. It was a mindless habit for him to run his arm through several motions. It was working perfectly and so he returned to his task of retracing Eldon 0821's tracks.

They walked silently for a long, long time, each lost in thought. Angus looked off in the distance, almost mesmerized. Gradually, a popping sound introduced itself in his environment. His eyes flickered acknowledgment and wonder. He consciously, gradually noticed the popping sound, much the same way someone swats in earnest at a pesky fly that only recently evoked some autonomic facial tics because of its trespasses.

Angus referred to his data screens. There were no anomalies indicated there. He looked up again. He looked around, turned his head, searching for the cause of that sound, the source.

There was nothing in their immediate surroundings that caught his attention. He looked out further. Nothing in the expanse ahead of them or the sky above seemed to produce that sound.

Angus was getting perplexed. *Where is that sound coming from?* he actually wondered. He tapped his helmet with one hand, the preferred troubleshooting method and time-honored tradition of the grunt and handyman. But the sound persisted.

"Monica?" Angus asked.

"Yes?"

"Do you hear that sound? It..." Angus said tentatively. They listened. Monica looked around as Angus had done. She too banged on her helmet. They both looked purplish as they trudged along, listening for the mysterious sound.

"What sound?" she asked. It had stopped. Neither one had heard it since Angus had asked her.

"A...popping sound," he tried to explain as they continued walking. His face registered different emotions, disappointment and frustration among them, as he tried to think of something else to tell her.

Instead, she listened. Closely. "No...Monica does not

hear an anomalous sound," she said.

Angus frowned. He listened,...

He listened very hard....

"It stopped," he finally concluded. "I can't hear it." He frowned again. It was gone. He gave up. They continued walking.

Minutes passed as did meters. They cut a straight line across their purple world.

POP.

POP.

He noticed it again; Aha! The popping sound coincided with their footsteps.

Almost. Angus stopped walking and let Monica continue walking. He watched her carefully. The sound actually coincided with her footsteps. She noticed that Angus had stopped. Monica stopped walking and turned around.

"What is it..." Monica asked.

"It stopped. Again." Angus said. Angus was confused. "The sound. It started again."

"And now it stopped again," he struggled to explain. They listened.

"It seemed to come from your footsteps," Angus said.

She too was confused. "Footsteps?" she asked.

"Start walking again." Angus ordered.

Unsure, she started walking again. Angus listened carefully and watched her intently. She walked around, purposefully, in a circle that brought her back to him.

"Negative." Monica said.

"Silence!" Angus blurted out in exasperation. He listened some more. Monica obligingly walked some more. Nothing. No popping sound. Angus was frustrated.

"Ach…" Angus muttered. "It's gone again."

She stopped walking. "Have you run a helmet diagnostic?" she asked.

"Yes. That's not it." Angus said as he scowled.

Angus grunted and continued walking again. Monica joined him and they continued quietly for some time.

*   *   *

Much later, Angus was concentrating on the land ahead. Eldon 0821's footprints reappeared in an area untouched by the cyclone. Up to this area they had been obliterated by the gale. And yet, this section looked as if drawn by a draughtsman. They were only slightly off of the line projected by Angus' faceplate. The line they drew was perfectly straight. POP!

Angus heard it. His eyes widened and he puffed his cheeks in exasperation and surprise.

POP!

There it was again. He was getting upset. Frustrated.

POP!

He determined to find the source this time. Furtively, he looked around, searching for that sound, like a hunter.

He looked at Monica's feet and studied them for many steps. Mystifyingly, the sound didn't always coincide with her steps.

He walked sideways now, his armored spacesuit was quite capable of obscure agility. This way he kept an eye on Monica while keeping up with her progress.

He raised his eyesight from her feet up her legs. It wasn't a problem with her knee joints. They moved irrespective of the popping.

His eyes moved up her legs to her hip joints. There was no correlation there either.

Her arms swung casually as she walked. But nothing indicated that they were the source of that noise. He raised his sight to her helmet. Her face. Her mouth.

She was opening and closing her lips at a consistent pace. Unconsciously, she was making that popping sound with her mouth.

Angus maneuvered in front of her, excitedly, and pointed at her accusingly with his huge augmented hand.

"It's you!" he declared.

She had been mesmerized and snapped out of it, startled. She stopped popping and took notice of him. "What?" Monica asked.

They stopped walking. "You are making that popping sound," Angus said.

She blinked at him, confused. "What?" Monica asked.

"You've been making that popping sound. All this

time. With your mouth." Angus spluttered, chasing the words out exasperatedly.

"Wha...Bu..." Monica spluttered in response. She looked lost. Angus shifted gears and accessed some files. He replayed video footage of her face and her mouth making the sound. He transferred it to her helmet, instantly.

She gaped at it. Nuances of expressions fluttered across her face: embarrassment, confusion, bashfulness. The corners of her mouth attempted a smile.

"Sorry...I..." Monica said.

"Well...." Angus stammered. He didn't know what to do. His face also fluctuated through a series of expressions and emotions. He attempted to say something, and then....

Started giggling.

She gaped at him as he made this strange new sound. He stared at her in silence and then giggled again.

She giggled too, almost in echo or response to him. It sounded insane, almost mechanical. Unpracticed.

And then she started laughing in earnest. This too was unpracticed, sounding more like hiccuping rather than laughter. But that changed as she laughed more.

Angus stared at her, fascinated by the rush of things. And then he too laughed, involuntarily. His laughter was no smoother or more natural than hers. But as they both laughed, it quickly sounded better, more natural, and this had the curious effect of making them laugh even more.

"...It...was...you," Angus spluttered and the laughter took them over. They laughed louder and harder. As each one laughed and hyperventilated and then caught their breath it made the other laugh even more. Uncontrollably.

Data screens in both of their helmets displayed alerts about their life signs, particularly their increasing respiration and their elevated levels of serotonins, endorphins and oxygen in their blood streams. The screens indicated these levels as they approached their individual red lines.

"I...didn't...know," Monica guffawed.

"It was you this whole time!" Angus bellowed.

Monica stopped abruptly, her eyes wide open and her mouth agape and then she shrieked and scrunched her eyes shut as she laughed even harder. The laughter came from the depths of their bodies.

They laughed so much and so hard that tears came to their eyes. After a moment the clean-up hoses in Angus' helmet shot out and sucked up the lose liquid.

The two of them stood in the middle of this violet blue desert laughing their heads off. Their arms swung carelessly as they hyperventilated and chortled. They stumbled around, two huge Colonial Militants being...

Silly.

Just over the horizon were two brilliant slivers, the slow twin planet-rise. They were clear of the horizon and intensely bright crescents. Their light was brilliant enough to banish the purple hue of the world. It was almost like daylight.

The crescents of the planets were partially broken up, striated by cirrus clouds in the distance. But this did not minimize their intensity, nor their beauty.

Angus and Monica's laughter died down gradually and naturally as the twins rose higher in the sky.

She was the first to notice them. "...Look!" she said in astonishment. They giggled as a residue of their jocularity and slowly subsided. A definite smile was on her face as she pointed at the sky.

Angus followed her indication and was struck by the sight of the planet-rise. The planets' atmospheres created amazing colors that shimmered with their own planet's atmosphere. They were both astonished.

"Have you ever seen anything like that?" Monica gasped, not exactly expecting an answer.

"Never..." Angus said and smiled, and then frowned as he hesitated. He stopped himself, because he faintly recalled that he had, many times. He looked at Monica for help.

"Yes! Haven't you?" he asked her. Monica's smile faltered as she thought about that. Her eyes glazed over as she tried to recall the past. She did remember and the more she thought about it the more she remembered.

"...uh...yes," she paused. "There is...some recollection." They looked at each other and acknowledged that they both had seen vistas of this kind before. The realization was stunning in its own simple way.

They turned back to the sky and stared for a long while. Angus concentrated, thinking. His attention drifted from the planets to another thought, or other thoughts. Monica continued smiling as she stared at the sky.

"Do you recall anything else?" Angus asked her.

That grabbed her attention away from the planets. She looked at him, thinking and nodding.

"...incomplete. Like a old data..." Monica said. Angus nodded. "Do you?" she asked.

"Yes, scrambled. I...remember seeing those planets like that. But not clearly..." Angus paused. "Not until you indicated them." Angus looked back at the sky.

"I remember many things..." he added.

His hand on the small of her back....

He sighed ruefully. They stood there for a long time watching the twin planets climb the sky and shrink away from the atmospheric distortion at the horizon.

Wordlessly, they turned back to their task and continued walking.

YET ANOTHER BATTLE

"It always ends the same way," Angus said.

Angus and Monica followed Eldon 0821's tracks across the plain. There were huge buttes on the horizon that seemed to watch their arduous trek in complete neutrality.

"Yes," Monica responded. As they walked, the plain ahead of them slowly started to look different. Further in the distance there were wisps of black smoke trailing into the air.

"All of them seem the same," Angus explained and they walked.

"Yes," she said and walked.

"Have you ever secured a Tower?" Angus asked her after many moments.

They walked further as she thought about her answer. "Uh...No," Monica ultimately responded. "There is no recollection of ever securing a Tower...

"...ever." The plain in the distance distracted Monica.

"I don't either," Angus said absentmindedly.

"But you destroyed one, didn't you, in the last battle we were in?" she pointed out, recalling that memory.

He nodded, abashed. "...I think that was a mistake," Angus confessed. "Maybe, I should have implemented a different tactical —"

"We are approaching smoke," Monica reported, interrupting him.

He looked up to see the smoke trailing off, in the distance. "Copy," Angus said.

As Angus and Monica walked, they slowly approached the edge of the plateau where the valley below finally revealed itself. In the distance what they saw was more smoke and a Tower complex. It was part of a particularly large tower complex.

As they got closer to the edge of the plateau, and more of the field in front of the Tower could be seen, what they also saw was a battle in progress.

Angus and Monica reached the edge and stopped. The battle was resolving itself. In the sky they saw the

Flying Vehicle picking off Attackers on the ground with its potent blasts, scaling their numbers down to a non-threatening size, neutralizing the attack.

It had been a very big battle. There were hundreds of damaged soldiers from both sides lying on the ground. The Attackers and Defenders were now the injured and dying.

They could see the Tower's Defenders giving up the battle, letting the Flying Vehicle fight it for them. While they watched, the Defenders turned and went back to the Tower.

The Attackers, one by one, were neutralized. Left to repair themselves or become scrap for the millions of repair crabs that would soon emerge.

Three,...two,...one.

The Flying Vehicle dropped the last Attacker. Another battle was over.

Monica stared out at the battlefield. The expression on her face was the antithesis of the wonder she experienced when they witnessed the twin planet-rise. She glanced at Angus. Angus was also staring at the battlefield. He too had the same sort of stunned expression she had, and if she could have seen herself, she would have known this.

She noticed when Angus' mouth dropped open. "What?" Monica asked.

Angus didn't respond.

"Angus?" Monica probed.

He blinked and then looked at her. She was nervous. He pointed at the Tower complex. Monica searched the battlefield. The Flying Vehicle circled the battlefield once more and then zoomed away over one of the hills behind the Tower. Angus was scrutinizing the valley floor. "There. See?" he pointed insistently.

She looked but hadn't identified whatever caught his attention.

"The OS17. The satellite link?" Angus explained apprehensively. This was incontrovertible evidence for Angus.

She looked at the Tower complex and quickly located a dish antenna on one of the higher points of the complex. She looked back at Angus who stood, considering her.

"Buddha?" Monica whispered. He nodded at her. Then they both nodded at each other solemnly before looking back at the entirety of the large Tower complex.

Together, Angus and Monica made a decision and moved forward as they descended from the plateau. Loose rocks preceded them as the littered battlefield jumbled closer. Despite their apparent clumsiness and the treachery of the terrain they kept their footing on the way down.

The landscape leveled out as they entered the battlefield proper. Dead soldiers lay all around them.

Many had been instantly destroyed and were left smoking, blackened husks, some of which were completely unidentifiable. Others were injured, some worse than others, either unconscious or wailing in their pain and suffering.

One soldier was screaming in pain and seemed to sustain his wailing despite his massive injuries. He continued as they passed and moved away from him. As they left him behind by several paces and maneuvered through the rest of the injured soldiers his screaming abruptly stopped. Exhaustion, shock or death silenced him.

Now the injured soldiers went into repair mode as Angus and Monica maneuvered among them. Millions of repair crabs emerged suddenly and scurried all over the place. The crabs' hissing movements rose from the whole valley like an anxious murmur that seemed to speak of regret and resignation after the battle.

Angus walked in a straight line. Monica looked around at the wreckage and carnage. It all made a great impression upon her. But Angus walked directly to the Tower complex walls, largely ignoring the ruins, fueled by the anger that filled him after they were almost killed by the cyclone. Monica couldn't tear her attention away from the battlefield as she trailed behind him.

Angus approached one set of doors that led into the Tower complex. The doors were closed and did not respond automatically when Monica and Angus approached them. He was forced to stop inches away from the closed doors, even though he motioned toward them as if he were entering. Frustrated, he stepped back and surveyed the complex. Monica watched him. Finally, he turned and walked in another direction.

Monica lingered, surveying the doors and walls for herself, and then followed Angus.

"This is the oxygenation section,..." Monica said, referring to her data screens that displayed a schematic of the complex.

"Yes," Angus answered.

"Where are you going?" Monica asked.

"Recon." She nodded and caught up to him. When in doubt, reconnaissance was always the prescribed procedure for any soldier. Together they found a building marked "B Wing". That side of the building had a series of huge, hangar-like doors.

Angus and Monica walked up to one of these larger doors. They too remained closed. Angus walked to a panel on the door frame and opened it. Inside was a lever: OPEN, CLOSE. He grabbed the lever and pulled it down.

The door opened and they walked into a large airlock system of two sets of doors that kept the lethal atmosphere out of the Tower complex. The second doors led them to a scene from Angus' dream that unfolded again as the doors slid open.

Inside the Tower complex there were several computer workstations, terminals, sprawling desks with several monitors embedded in them. At one of these terminals (as well as throughout the complex), the computer monitors began flashing a display:

◇◇

ACTIVITY IN B WING; RECEIVING!

◇◇

Buddha had noticed.

The receiving area was a huge space, metal everywhere. A flicker of recognition clouded Angus' face. Ahead of where they stood was the assembly room. Angus could see the armor-building machines in the distance through another threshold. "...I remember this place,..." Angus whispered.

Monica barely heard him as she considered the area. Angus turned to look at her. "Don't you?" he asked.

She stopped and, after a while, nodded slowly. Angus turned and walked into the assembly room. As he entered, Angus stared at the platforms, at the strange, yet familiar, equipment. These were the armor-building machines, the contraptions that took the young versions of Angus, Monica and countless others and encased them and augmented them in their armored environment suits that would be their homes for the rest of their lives. Angus remembered. Although everything was dormant, he gazed at the machinery, unsure if it was making noise or if he was simply recalling sounds from long ago. The static robotic arms clanged and buzzed in Angus' mind. The conveyor belts and conduits hummed and rattled, even though they too sat still. The tranquil space was thrumming with imagined noise.

He climbed one of the platforms and walked around to get a better view of the area. Monica was also remembering, as she stood staring agape at everything. "What is this?" she asked.

"This is where...we were assembled." he said quietly. Monica walked around. There were multiple rows of machines and each row stretched for a long distance to both sides. The platform had multiple catwalks that stretched out to the back of the huge room, allowing access, up and down, to all of the machinery kept there. Monica made her way across one catwalk and explored the back rows.

Angus climbed down from the platform to the ground floor. He moved about in a daze, overwhelmed by the experience of being in the middle of these novel, yet familiar, devices. This ground floor was the foundation for all these machines. The actual work was done one level above where the machines lined up with the conveyor belts and movers that transferred the young soldiers from station to station. Standing among these machines, Angus felt dwarfed as they loomed over him.

The access way was cramped for Angus' standards, but he navigated through the area easily enough.

Monica gazed at the area, lost in thought. She, too, heard echoes, faint sounds, memories of being in this room as a young woman. The whole experience had begun as she came through a set of doors with the hundreds of others who were also processed at that time. She saw those doors at the far end of the assembly room as she turned to look.

She descended from the platform and approached the doors where Angus joined her. She stepped toward a door and opened it. What was revealed behind the doors took their breath away: dormitories.

After a moment Angus and Monica stepped inside. They walked onto a deck that stretched to either side, like the platform in the assembly room.

On the opposite side of the deck was a row of hundreds of elevators. Angus and Monica stood between two elevators at a railing and looked out at a metal lattice of levels about thirty feet from them. Each level was arrayed with hundreds of translucent capsules, each of which held sleeping human bodies.

Angus and Monica stared at the lattice work in disbelief. There was a level directly in front of them and several levels above and below; at least half of this section of the building was constructed underground.

"What is this..." Monica asked, but she didn't really

need an answer as her expression suggested a fair amount of recognition. The entire place was virtually silent. Only low hums and trills from support systems that carried out their automatic functions filled the area. That changed suddenly.

As they watched, one section of dormitories came to life with the sounds of hundreds of motors. The capsules popped open. Hundreds of adolescent men and women stood up, in almost perfect synchronization, climbed out of the capsules and fell in line as they started to shuffle out of the dormitory in one direction.

"New soldiers," Angus sighed. Monica glanced at him, understanding despite a basic resistance to the idea. The files of young vulnerable-looking soldiers threaded past them into the assembly room where they presented themselves to the vast network of machinery there. The assembly room came alive with all of the machinery rumbling into operation throughout the area. Angus and Monica looked back and forth at the queueing soldiers as they made their way into the assembly room.

Angus abruptly turned around and left the dormitories. "Where are you going?" Monica asked. Angus moved away swiftly, forcing her to match his pace and catch up to him.

"Looking for a terminal," he explained. Monica blinked confusion back at him. *Why would he want a terminal?* The new soldiers mostly ignored them as

Monica followed Angus back into the assembly room.

Near one of the countless assembly machines inside the assembly room Angus found a terminal and sat on one of the chair-like contraptions designed for Colonial Militants. He plugged into the terminal in the same way he did on the forgotten, crashed transport ship out in the wastelands.

"Why?" Monica asked.

"See what is happening with those new soldiers," Angus explained. A console screen reacted to him and a menu appeared.

But it was the computer voice over the area's public address system that acknowledged Angus the most by saying, "Hi, Angus 7873. May I help you?" This computer voice was similar to that of the computer on the transport ship. Angus made an immediate mental inquiry as he had done on the ship. "What would you like to know about new soldiers?" the computer inquired.

Angus made another silent inquiry. "I'm sorry. Cannot find directory. Access denied," the computer declared neutrally.

Monica noticed that one of the other displays on the console was flashing an alert:

ANOMALOUS ACTIVITY SOURCE LOCATED!

Assembly Room: Console 77483

Angus tried again. "What would you like to know about new Colonial Militia?" the computer asked helpfully. Angus made another instant mental inquiry.

"ANGUS 7873, what are you doing?" Buddha asked, booming in a distinct and intimidating voice over the PA system.

Angus froze. Shocked. Frightened. He caught his breath. Monica was also shocked. Buddha's voice was completely different from the computer voice. It didn't bother to be polite. Instead, it sounded impatient, busy.

"Buddha," Monica gasped, her comprehension was instant. She looked to Angus to see what he was going to do. However, he was still frozen in shock. The look on his face frightened Monica, so much so that she reached out, instinctively and touched him in an age-old attempt to make contact and communicate. "Angus?" she said.

"ANGUS 7873, what are you doing? RESPOND NOW!" Buddha ordered again.

Monica glanced at the alert in the other screen and made a decision. She disconnected Angus from the terminal. He snapped back with a gasp.

"Move," she said.

"What?"

"We have to go. Buddha knows you're here," she urged Angus.

Angus suddenly understood and nodded. He stood and gathered his wits as she tugged on him. They turned and ran back through the huge assembly room on their way out to the battlefield.

The assembly room was busy with activity that shocked and stunned Angus. Each new reminder of their origins affected Angus more than Monica. Back at the transport ship, after he had found himself all alone, he had made his discovery without warning or preparation. That information was a revelation as well as an assault. Not to say that Monica wasn't affected by reliving the moments when she was encased forever in her armored suit, but Angus had exposed her to the information with more forethought. He had eased her into it. Nonetheless, she and Angus fought their emotions and reactions as they ran through the maze of machines that were doing the same thing to all of these seemingly voluntary new soldiers that had been done to them.

The conveyor belts, robotic arms and assembly machines literally took these young bodies, positioned them as necessary and sealed them away in their shiny new armor. Some couldn't help but react in terror as they were manipulated and processed. Angus and Monica forcibly remembered their own experiences.

By the time Angus and Monica reached the receiving area, before coming to the air-lock doors, they were now among brand new Colonial Militants, just off the assembly line, who were ready for their first mission orders. Most of these soldiers were stunned and frightened by this experience, but their suits' cybernetic emotional dampeners were taking care of that as they lined up for service.

Angus and Monica made it through these new Colonial Militants and started to process through the air-lock's double doors. As they waited for the doors to function Monica glanced at one of the Colonial Militants beside her, a shiny brand new young female soldier. Monica caught her breath as she stared at the young soldier's face. This soldier was a younger version of Monica, cloned from the same strain as she had been, and Monica vaguely recognized her. Without looking away, Monica silently reached out and tapped Angus' armor, getting his attention. He glanced at her, unaware of why she had drawn his attention until she glanced at him and pointed at Rachel 2020. Angus saw the "family resemblance" immediately and then glanced at the other soldiers around them. Monica and Angus looked at each other in quick recognition of what they were passing: shiny new copies of their former selves. Not just new Colonial Militants, but new clones. As the air-lock cycled, they were deposited in the bright outdoors, forced to leave that thought behind for now.

Outside, Calvin 6501 was walking from the Tower to B Wing, the last known location of Angus 7873, according to the information he had been relayed. He saw Angus and Monica as they ran out of the huge doors from B

Wing. They ran through the battlefield the way they had come, back up to the plateau. Calvin 6501 immediately raised his laser cannon and fired a warning shot.

Angus and Monica were startled to see it pass by them. They stopped to identify the source of the shot. They located Calvin 6501 very quickly. "Stop! Identify designation!" Calvin 6501 ordered.

Angus shook his head at Monica. She already understood. He gestured toward the fallen soldiers surrounding them. They scrambled around the injured soldiers and stopped. They crouched down and hid from Calvin 6501.

Calvin 6501 trudged onto the battlefield, swinging his cannon back and forth, ready to fire again. He scanned the bodies lying about. Angus and Monica were kneeling next to three or four soldiers in repair mode. Their own data screens displayed all the data transmitted by those bodies. They were in a confusing field of distinctive data.

As Calvin 6501 got closer to Monica and Angus, he looked right at them but didn't shoot. He could see them, but he couldn't see them...Calvin 6501 saw the mass of conflicting data. Most of the objects were fallen and dead soldiers, non-transmitting yet identifiable outlines of Colonial Militants, or even parts of them. The others were in repair mode and did transmit some identifications. Angus and Monica were identifiable but they had turned off their complete identifications back at the downed transport. With their disabled ENET-1s, they were just objects, not soldiers. Angus slowly placed a restraining hand on Monica's arm.

Angus then turned off his suit; his lights and screens powered down completely. Monica was surprised and looked at him quizzically. He nodded emphatically for her to follow his example. She powered down her own suit as Calvin 6501 got closer. He stopped within ten feet of them and scanned them. Repair crabs from the battlefield climbed onto Angus and Monica; deactivated, they too were now potential salvage.

Calvin 6501's data screen showed him a layout of the soldiers around him:

```
HENDERSON.....rm >>¬XC ^   5^%%
WILL.......rm < ∃ *** ^ ^ ^
KOHL......dead *** < ** > ^^ B
(blank)
(blank)
TIGHE.......rm * ^^\^^^ ^ ^ /\
```

The blank slots were Angus and Monica, seen as physical bodies, just like rocks, terrain or dead soldiers, but not as active Colonial Militants. Calvin 6501 couldn't and didn't recognize them. Firing on inert soldiers didn't make much sense right now.

Angus' own repair crabs came out now and seemed to have a discussion with the general nosy crabs. Some started taking apart Angus' repaired arm while his own repair crabs tried to prevent them from doing so.

Calvin 6501 scanned the area again. He was looking right at them but he couldn't isolate them in his data screens.

"Identify designation!" Calvin 6501 ordered again.

He could see Angus and Monica looking back at him; he was staring into their eyes. More anxious than Angus, Monica moved her head, eyes and mouth. Angus, however, remained still. But Calvin 6501 didn't seem to get what any of that meant. He just stared at them, blankly, swinging his cannon back and forth over them, perfectly capable of delivering a lethal shot to both of them.

Angus and Monica were barely breathing as they crouched there. With their suits deactivated, their ventilation systems were off for the time being. Their faceplates were fogging up despite their attempts at subterfuge. Angus and Monica waited patiently.

Then some of the first rehabilitated soldiers began to get up around the battlefield, drawing Calvin 6501's attention. In one move he gave up staring at Angus and Monica, turned around and headed to the B Wing doors. Angus and Monica both breathed sighs of relief and watched him reach the doors and go back inside.

"That was Calvin 6501," Angus said, muffled through his deactivated suit.

"What?" Monica muffled back.

Angus powered up his suit. The foreign crabs stopped

working abruptly now that the suit was clearly operational. Angus' crabs seemed miffed and snatched parts back from the nosy crabs and undid their "repairs."

Monica powered up too. The crabs scuttled off her.

"That was Calvin 6501," Angus explained.

She could hear him clearly now.

"Yes..." Monica said, not understanding his point.

"Do you remember him?" Angus asked.

Monica thought about it and shook her head.

"We were with him. At the last battle we fought," Angus said.

She couldn't remember. He stood up and started walking toward the slope. "Let's go," he said.

She stood and followed him. "Where are we going?" Monica asked.

"To watch from the plateau," he explained. They weaved around the bodies. Monica looked at the soldiers and the crabs busily at work. Her data screens identified all of the soldiers:

```
STEVEN.....rm ^^ * ++ |+ +
DOBEN......rm || | \\ ^ (**
SUZE.....rm /OO - | \\//
```

Monica slowed down. "Angus," Monica called to him. He looked at her.

Monica stopped walking, looking at all of the soldiers. "Can you patch into these repair mode soldiers?"

she asked.

He stopped walking and turned around to look at the soldiers. He referred to his data screens in his helmet. He looked back at her with an expression of intrigue.

"Yes?..." he said, cluing in. He knelt down by one of the soldiers and checked him out. "We can patch in and..."

"...neutralize their ENET-1 microprocessors," Monica finished his sentence.

A genuine smile crossed his face as he nodded more and more enthusiastically at her. After a moment it was infectious and she couldn't help but smile (a child's first accomplishment acknowledged, perhaps).

In the assembly room, Calvin 6501 was still looking for Angus and Monica. He had his laser cannon out, swinging back and forth. He found Terminal 77483 and plugged in.

The console screens displayed information he already had:

LOCATE ANGUS 7873

Last location: Assembly Room,
Console 77483

Calvin 6501 seemed to understand his latest orders and continued looking for them.

Monica was studying one soldier on a data screen:

Subject: Suze 4252
Reset ENET-1?
No.

Both Angus and Monica were plugged into two different soldiers. As soon as they finished with one, they moved to another. Angus plugged in and....:

Subject: Peter 2543
Reset ENET-1?
No.

Calvin 6501 walked around the assembly machines looking for them. Even though he had been looking right at Angus and Monica outside on the battlefield, that meant nothing to him. What did mean something to him was their last known location, particularly according to Buddha. Whereas he trusted Buddha, he didn't trust his own eyes. His default subroutine was to retrace their steps from that last known location — a logically sound approach, but a faulty one.

However, Buddha had escalated its interest:

DEFENDERS ON ALERT; LOCATE ANGUS 7873

Locate Colonial Militant not
transmitting recognition code.

This was slightly more information for Calvin 6501 and he seemed to comprehend it. He therefore stopped his search indoors, turned and headed outside. But now everyone would be looking for Angus.

Angus and Monica scurried around from soldier to soldier and disabled their ENET-1 microprocessors. "Fourteen soldiers will be one hundred percent in ten minutes, so far," Monica reported.

"Good," Angus answered.

One of the huge B Wing doors opened and Calvin 6501 came out and headed directly onto the battlefield. Calvin 6501's data screen indicated the status of the fallen soldiers all around him as he looked for Angus. More and more of them were approaching completely rehabilitated status and would be potent threats if they designated as Attackers.

Almost as a provocation, the long array of B Wing doors opened at the same time. Framed in these doors were the regrouped Defenders, standing at attention and apparently ready for another battle.

Computer screens at workstations throughout the complex flashed a new alert:

DEFENDERS ACTIVE; LOCATE ANGUS 7873

Locate Colonial Militant not
transmitting recognition code.
Locate Angus 7873
NEUTRALIZE!

This alert was immediately received by all Defenders. In fact, all of the operational Colonial Militants in the area were alerted.

The Defenders took a step outside and raised their laser cannons to firing positions. The whole line took another step, and then another, and then they spread out following basic procedures as they deployed on the battlefield again. Right behind them was another line of Defenders waiting for them to clear the way so that they too could deploy.

Monica disconnected from a soldier, stood up and moved to another one. As she did so, she noticed the emerging Defenders. She paused for a moment, "Angus?"

"What?" he asked as he worked on another soldier. He looked at her when she didn't respond. Instead she pointed.

"Defenders," she said without taking her eyes off the line of soldiers. Angus shifted his position and saw them. The second line was spreading out directly behind the first line of Defenders, doubling their breadth. Each soldier waved his weapon back and forth across their field of fire, searching for targets.

"But they can't see us," she said, not entirely certain.

"Yet," Angus concluded. As he scanned the area filling with Defenders he noticed one soldier in front of all of them. He stood to get a better look.

Calvin 6501 noticed something on his data screen:

"Angus 7873. Located," Calvin 6501 reported, thanks to his new data.

Not only did Angus and Monica see Calvin 6501's data screen in their helmets but they heard him as well. "Angus..." Monica hissed at him.

"Vector seven two six,..." Calvin 6501 reported to everyone concerned.

"Keep working," Angus urged Monica. She paused and then hurried to another soldier as Angus crouched back down and tried to evade Calvin 6501, but Calvin 6501 fired his laser. The beam hit just in front of Angus, vaporizing the sand and debris in a large ball of energy. Angus ducked behind the soldier he was repairing. He pivoted and fired back at Calvin 6501.

Calvin 6501 ducked automatically. He plotted a more accurate target based on Angus' line of fire.

Knowing this, Angus ran for cover. Another explosion occurred immediately behind Angus. The soldier he had been repairing received a direct hit and was destroyed. The repair crabs were caught off guard by the shooting. They tended to only come out when fighting was over. Now, they scrambled for cover.

The battlefield was pocked with hundreds of old craters from all of the explosions of previous battles. Angus scrambled into what amounted to a deep gully, literally a series of craters that formed a large gouge.

Calvin 6501 lost Angus momentarily. Monica recovered from the same blast and hurried to another soldier.

Another laser blast hit a few feet away from Angus. He glanced in its direction. The Defenders had seen him. There were about fifty of them and they all started firing at Angus.

Angus hunkered down in the hole as laser fire sprayed across the top throwing sand and debris over him. The air around him sizzled from the crisscrossing beams. Monica was frightened by the onslaught directed at Angus.

The Defenders started to flank Angus as they pinned him down. They swung out to their left, and continued shooting at him.

Out in front Calvin 6501 was nearing Angus.

Angus crawled along the gully looking for another hiding place since all of the fire was concentrated in one area. He reached a gap from which he could see Calvin 6501. He aimed and fired at him and hit Calvin 6501 on the arm, knocking him off his feet.

Angus took the opportunity to climb out of the hole and ran for another crater nearby. Some of the Defenders noticed and adjusted their aim. At the last moment a laser bolt glanced off Angus, giving him a helpful shove into the new crater.

Before Monica disconnected from the soldier she was currently administering she made another adjustment. A menu appeared on her data screen. She scrolled down to a specific item: ATTACK MODE! Then she disconnected and ran to the side.

Angus rolled over on his side, surveying the damage he had suffered. He was relatively okay; an armor plate had been torn to shreds. The Defenders continued their fire as they searched for him.

Calvin 6501 was back on his feet and advancing. His data screens indicated the terrain, the crater and the outline of Angus hiding. He advanced. Soon he would have a clean shot. He aimed in anticipation.

Angus looked over the rim of the crater. Calvin 6501 was aiming at him. He ducked back down just as a laserbolt hit Calvin 6501.

Monica had fired at Calvin 6501 and fired again. She hit him again, but this one glanced off him as he fell. She swung around and shot at the advancing Defenders. She hit several of them, interrupting their shooting.

Monica's first shot had gone through Calvin 6501's shoulder. On the ground, where he lay, he struggled to make it work. He stood again and scanned in her direction. He knew he had been targeted by another soldier against whom he hadn't defended. He spotted her. "Second non-transmitting Attacker located. Vector four four seven,..." he alerted Buddha.

This time Angus shot at Calvin 6501, making him duck.

Some Defenders turned, looking for Monica. She ran from her original location, trying to avoid their fire. Some spotted her and fired as she ran. Her huge armored suit moving fluidly, she dove into a ditch and rolled. She sat up and looked out. They had missed her.

The soldier she had adjusted as an Attacker sat up, fully rehabilitated. Instantly he turned around, located the Defenders and started shooting. One of the Defenders exploded — a direct hit. Two more went down thanks to his fire.

Monica aimed and launched a grenade. She launched another. They landed in front of the Defenders.

One of them stepped right onto the first one when it exploded, taking his legs off and flipping him backwards into the air.

The second grenade detonated, disabling three more Defenders.

The other Defenders launched three grenades at Monica. She scrambled out of the hole and ran for another one. She reached it as the first grenade blew. Then the second. And the third.

The repaired Attacker launched a grenade at the Defenders. He ran to the side, away from their return fire.

The grenade exploded. Five Defenders were hit directly and destroyed.

From her hiding place, Monica peered at the Defenders and realized that they included the newly processed Colonial Militants they had seen inside B Wing; she recognized Rachel 2020 from the distance.

Inside the Tower complex, display screens very quickly scrolled down to the following stages:

AIR SUPPORT ACTIVE

LAUNCH AIR SUPPORT

Elsewhere in the Tower complex there was a hangar. Its ceiling doors opened to allow the deployment of the Flying Vehicle. It powered up and disengaged from its power sources and couplings. It took off and left the hangar.

The Flying Vehicle zipped into the airspace over the new fighting. It circled the battlefield slowly looking for rogue fugitives, two to be precise.

More soldiers rehabilitated by Monica and Angus, having completed their repair routines, stood and engaged the battle. At first they hesitated, studying the situation, but in a moment they switched over to attack mode, given the circumstances. They stood up in different places spread out through the battlefield. They provided a confusing new element for the

Defenders to consider.

Four newly repaired soldiers stood and fired their laser cannons at the deployed Defenders. The Defenders took heavy casualties. The Flying Vehicle circled the battlefield again, reconsidering this new development.

"Angus. Report!" Monica yelled. Angus turned to look for Monica. He was still in the crater.

"Nominal. And you?" he responded.

"Nominal," she responded.

"The Flying Vehicle is active and engaged," he told her.

She knew, of course, but she looked anyway. "Copy," she said.

Now there were a total of seven repaired soldiers, spread out through the area, fighting the Defenders. The Defenders were shooting at Angus and Monica with everything they had.

Five more Defenders fell. Another Defender fired on them. She hit a repaired soldier in the helmet and blasted it apart. That soldier fell backward, dead.

Monica looked back at Angus. Calvin 6501 was spraying a stream of laserfire toward Angus, sweeping closer to him. "ANGUS!" Monica yelled.

Angus launched a grenade at Calvin 6501. It hit his laser cannon in the trigger section and got lodged there, causing the cannon to misfire and explode, throwing sparks and spewing smoke.

But the grenade remained stuck. Calvin 6501 looked at it, tried to shake it off and looked up at Angus. Their eyes met. Calvin 6501 knew. Angus grimaced.

The grenade exploded, ripping Calvin 6501's right arm, side and his head apart. Angus climbed out of the crater and hurried to Calvin 6501's remains. Immediately it reminded him of Roach 9901's gruesome remains. He looked like a broken egg seeping yoke from its core.

Angus glanced at Calvin 6501's helmet, nearby, and froze. Calvin 6501's helmet remained intact while his head had been pulled off of his body. It now lay on its side in the bloody bottom of the helmet, where it came to rest. It was turned to face Angus. His eyes were open and his mouth was frozen in a death gasp. He looked surprised.

"Calvin!..." Angus blurted out. Without reason or meaning, Angus' eyes teared up.

"Calvin?" he said as if hoping to get a response.

None came.

THE END

Throughout the Tower complex computer screens flashed:

◇◇

ENGAGE AIR SUPPORT!
ENGAGE AIR SUPPORT!

◇◇

The Flying Vehicle changed its attitude from hunt to kill and started dropping laser bolts throughout the battlefield. Angus was forced to leave Calvin and run for another hole. A bolt missed him, barely. The newly repaired soldiers got hit one by one as the Flying Vehicle identified them. The beams cut three of them down.

Monica saw that the Flying Vehicle was resolving the

battle so quickly from its strategically superior position. She saw Angus run from one crater to another, moving his huge mass with amazing agility. The Flying Vehicle hovered above them altering its position with minute adjustments. She took aim and fired at it.

It dodged and immediately fired back at her, instantly calculating return fire. The beam missed and hit dirt, but the shock-wave threw her back.

More repaired soldiers woke up only to get hit by the enemy fire as soon as they went to attack mode.

A beam chased Angus out of one crater into another one.

Monica sat up and saw her first repaired soldier fire at the Flying Vehicle. He hit it on its side. The ship seemed to shrug it off and then shot back at him, landing a direct hit.

The soldier exploded. The beam pulverized him, throwing debris everywhere. Monica gaped at the remains as smoke billowed in a black column with the Tower standing behind it. As the thick smoke cleared, she saw the dish antenna on the top of one of the buildings.

She searched for Angus on the battlefield. Angus was launching grenades, creating diversions so that he could then run for it. BOOM. BOOM. BOOM, BOOM. BOOM. The grenades exploded in order as Angus maneuvered around the battle.

Monica checked her cannon. Rockets! Her cache

was empty; she was out of them. She grabbed a nearby repairing soldier and turned her over by hoisting her massive frame. Rockets! She grabbed one from the soldier's cache. As she grabbed it, it was backwards in her grip. Without thinking, she flipped it in mid-air, caught it — with some panache — and immediately loaded it in her own launcher.

Monica carefully aimed at the dish antenna and locked on target.

The Flying Vehicle pivoted, evaluating the overall situation.

Monica fired.

The Flying Vehicle had recommitted to chasing Angus again, but part of its attention was on Monica's actions.

Monica's rocket snaked through the air and drew a line right for the antenna. It hit it straight on. The antenna shattered.

The beams chased Angus and cut through other soldiers on the ground as he ran to another crater.

Angus stumbled and rolled into a crater. His vision speckled with spots and colored lights — *His hand on the small of her back* — and the persistent residual memory of some forgotten love. He shuddered to a stop, shook his head and stared at a Defender aiming right at his heart.

Eldon 0821 was part of the flanking maneuver of Defenders from the Tower complex, placing him directly in front of Angus. His shiny new armor was now marred with corroded plates and parts salvaged from the battlefield. He had received extensive repair after the previous battle (probably Eldon 0821's first).

Angus gaped at Eldon 0821's youthful face, bringing his cannon up in response. There was a flicker of something there — recognition? — as Eldon 0821 hesitated before delivering a lethal blast.

Time seemed to slow down as Angus also hesitated from pulling his trigger and firing on Eldon. He couldn't. Angus recalled looking at Eldon when they first met, from almost the same proximity. He also recalled seeing his own reflection back in the transport.

Angus cringed, waiting for the lethal blast as the Flying Vehicle's beams caught up, behind him, in the crater.

The beams stopped. The Flying Vehicle stopped shooting. It was hovering over Angus' new position as he stared up at it. It made tiny adjustments to its position in mid-air, from where it could have destroyed Angus with one shot.

In the Flying Vehicle's cockpit, its own screens were a jumble of data:

```
    ``/`/ v *`* f --12`3`439 ^^
         z9*#a#a~~~```
 k8w8** rf9aj**/7<<<.8 >> . > \7//\.x
```

The screen flickered. Re-established. The Flying

Vehicle started to circle the battlefield again; it had to re-plot the battleground. The Flying Vehicle's screen now had new information:

```
◇◇◇◇◇◇◇◇◇◇◇◇◇◇◇◇◇◇◇◇◇◇◇◇◇◇◇◇◇◇◇◇◇◇◇◇◇◇◇◇◇◇◇◇◇◇◇◇◇◇◇◇◇◇◇◇◇

        SWITCHING TO ONBOARD SYSTEM!

          Telemetry interruption.
◇◇◇◇◇◇◇◇◇◇◇◇◇◇◇◇◇◇◇◇◇◇◇◇◇◇◇◇◇◇◇◇◇◇◇◇◇◇◇◇◇◇◇◇◇◇◇◇◇◇◇◇◇◇◇◇◇
```

It had lost the Attacker/Defender designations and had to determine them all over again on its own, without Buddha's help.

But more importantly, Buddha was surprised! Computer screens throughout the Tower complex were flashing one alert:

```
◇◇◇◇◇◇◇◇◇◇◇◇◇◇◇◇◇◇◇◇◇◇◇◇◇◇◇◇◇◇◇◇◇◇◇◇◇◇◇◇◇◇◇◇◇◇◇◇◇◇◇◇◇◇◇◇◇

        TELEMETRY INTERRUPTION
        TELEMETRY INTERRUPTION
        TELEMETRY INTERRUPTION
◇◇◇◇◇◇◇◇◇◇◇◇◇◇◇◇◇◇◇◇◇◇◇◇◇◇◇◇◇◇◇◇◇◇◇◇◇◇◇◇◇◇◇◇◇◇◇◇◇◇◇◇◇◇◇◇◇
```

Angus sat up and looked around after realizing that he was still intact and operational. "MONICA? MONICA?" he called out anxiously.

Monica looked at him. "Copy. Here," she said.

"Excellence! Excellence!" he gasped and slouched back down in his hiding place. After catching his breath and the rest of his wits, he laughed. "That was...great!" he cheered.

"Yes, yes. Great. Roger. Great!" she agreed,

unaccustomed to elation but in complete agreement, nonetheless. She looked around and grinned. The Defenders stood around, lost. More soldiers got up after their repair routines were completed. They too were lost. None of them had clear designations of Attacker or Defender and therefore had no immediate purposes.

Angus scrambled out of the crater, stood up, glanced at Eldon and ran over to Monica. He studied the battlefield as she emerged from her cover. He reached her and impulsively hugged her, metal clanking and grinding on metal. She didn't know what to do, but smiled nonetheless.

They parted and looked around at the battlefield. Monica had a big, unpracticed smile on her face. She looked at Angus.

Angus was beaming. He held up his thumbs. "Excellence!"

The Flying Vehicle's screens flashed a new alert:

◇◇

RETURN TO HANGAR/AWAITING ORDER!

◇◇

No one was fighting and Buddha gave no instructions. Since it too had no immediate purpose, the Flying Vehicle turned and left the battlefield to wait for a new set of orders.

No one and nothing listened to Buddha. Throughout the Tower complex's many terminals and computer screens the same alert flashed:

◇◇

TELEMETRY INTERRUPTION

◇◇

Without the antenna connection the Colonial Militants were unaware of Buddha's anxiety.

On the battlefield Angus and Monica were amidst the confused and repaired soldiers wandering around in a daze. They were the only two cheering, but some of the Colonial Militants closest to them couldn't help but make strange, sympathetic facial expressions as they witnessed Angus and Monica in their jubilation.

Angus stopped with an idea. "Monica!" She looked at him and he was already hurrying back into the Tower complex. She turned to follow him.

Inside, Angus plugged into the first terminal he found. "ANGUS 7873, what are you doing?" Buddha asked, resounding in the big space.

"Can you stop belligerent operations?" Angus asked. Monica joined him and stared at the computer screens on the workstation.

"Yes." Buddha said, impatiently and simply.

"Have you received GCS Order 8685.335?" Angus inquired. Despite Buddha's pushy demeanor, it was still a computer and responded as one when queried.

"Accessing GCS Order 8685.335. Yes, GCS Order 8685.335, received and processed," Buddha said.

So Buddha knew, Angus thought for a long while. Monica had caught on as well. The fighting, just like this last battle, had carried on this whole time while Buddha had known about the cancellation of operations on CEM.4, this angry red orb. After all, its purpose was the administration of battles, not the determination of whether or not to wage war. That was a decision that should have been made by someone else.

Angus got an idea. It might not work, but he tried it anyway. "Stop..." he blurted out. Monica looked at him apprehensively.

"Stop all belligerent operations and tactics for all Colonial Militants on CEM.4 until further notice from GCS," Angus instructed Buddha. Monica caught her breath and looked at Angus in surprise. Angus looked at Monica anxiously as Buddha processed the command and they waited nervously.

"Stopping belligerent operations until further notice," Buddha responded obediently. Angus and Monica smiled at each other with a bemused combination of surprise and confusion; Buddha was a computer.

*　　*　　*

With some tiny exceptions, fidgeting and shifting, the Colonial Militants on the battlefield and throughout the rest of the Tower complex waited right where they were. Without Buddha's acknowledgment to their reports of one hundred percent rehabilitation, they had no instructions to join up with other soldiers or wander the planet in search of a battle. They just waited as the day went by.

The repair crabs, however, had their own purpose and default instructions. They carried out repairs as usual and salvaged those parts that could be used again from the dead and destroyed soldiers littered on the battlefield.

Angus and Monica had been at the workstation during that whole time. Both had connected to the Terminal, helping each other in their negotiations with Buddha. The computer screen on the terminal indicated what Angus was accessing:

```
TOWER LAYOUT:
Communication/Telemetry
Cooling
Ground level
Maintenance
Mining
Power
Reactor
REFINERY
Repair
```

He selected and accessed "REFINERY."

Now their relationship with Buddha was much like their relationship with the ship computer on the downed transport. Angus or Monica thought and Buddha responded.

"Powering up refinery," Buddha confirmed.

They went down several checklists according to the computer. They made sure that the reactor was ready. Then they checked if there was raw material in the refinery.

Finally they turned on the Tower. "Powering up tower. Plant status: active. Plant integrity: 100%. Refinery status: active. Processing," Buddha reported.

The basic nature of the entire Tower complex changed suddenly. Whereas it had been this largely silent and dormant group of buildings, it now was a busy factory intent on a variety of activities. Lights and sounds filled the area indicating the various chores that were being carried out by all of the different sectors in the complex.

Conveyor belts and sorters moved tons of soil through the processors. Repair and service robots of all kinds and sizes scurried around, administering to the processes at work. All of the machinery led to the height of the Tower. That was where the end product would turn out.

The battlefield had been cleared of dead and injured soldiers by the usual crab repair activity. And now, with new instructions from Angus and Monica, there were soldiers walking around the whole area.

Repair crabs were also working on the dish antenna Monica shot. One of them, P-Vo, looked up as the Flying Vehicle passed overhead, with new instructions of its own.

The Flying Vehicle's screen displayed a whole new alert:

◇◇◇

ALL COLONIAL MILITIA!

HEAD TO PLANT # 1

◇◇◇

Helpful diagrams were transmitted as well by the Flying Vehicle to all of the soldiers, letting them know exactly how to find their way to Plant #1.

Angus and Monica came outside through the Tower doors as the Flying Vehicle reached far out toward the horizon.

As the hours became days, the plain peppered with tiny dots of thousands of soldiers who were the nearest to the Tower complex, returning from wandering the planet surface. They were all converging on the Tower complex.

Angus and Monica walked out to the center of the former battlefield. Some other soldiers also followed them out, lieutenants they had promoted in the process. Eldon was one of them. They stopped and turned around.

They looked up at the Tower. A huge puffy clean white plume was growing out of the top.

Angus and Monica looked at each other and smiled.

They looked up at the sky. The oxygenated vapor flowed into the atmosphere. It mixed with the new clouds that now were there and created a majestic turbulence.

While they watched, a rainbow appeared in the plume. A light rain started to fall. And a little patch of revealed sky slowly turned blue.

Angus turned to Monica, smiling, and said to her, "Look for the blue sky!"

Melton Eduardo Cartes is an art director/designer
in advertising and an animator/illustrator. He has written
over twenty-five feature-length screenplays, three of
which reached the semifinals in two different contests,
twice in the Austin Film Festival and once in the Nicholl
Fellowships. He wrote, produced and directed
a short subject entitled ROY'S HEART that can be
seen on YouTube. He recently formed an animation
studio called AlbinoPigGorilla Studio with two fellow
animators. He currently lives in Oakland, California.

9 780578 405773